TELL IT TRUE

TELL IT TRUE

Tim Lockette

TRIANGLE
SQUARE
books for young readers

Seven Stories Press
New York • Oakland • London

A TRIANGLE SQUARE BOOK FOR YOUNG READERS
PUBLISHED BY SEVEN STORIES PRESS

SEVEN STORIES PRESS
140 Watts Street
New York, NY 10013
www.sevenstories.com

College professors and high school and middle school teachers
may order free examination copies of Seven Stories Press titles.
Visit https://www.sevenstories.com/pg/resources-academics
or email academics@sevenstories.com.

Library of Congress Cataloging-in-Publication Data

Names: Lockette, Tim, author.
Title: Tell it true / Tim Lockette.
Description: New York, NY : Seven Stories Press, [2021] | Audience: Ages
10-14. | Summary: A high school outcast finds herself in charge of the
school newspaper and as she navigates the dilemmas, challenges and
unintended consequences of journalism, she finds her life--and her
convictions--changing in ways she could not have imagined.
Identifiers: LCCN 2021016598 (print) | LCCN 2021016599 (ebook) | ISBN
9781644210826 (hardcover) | ISBN 9781644210833 (ebook)
Subjects: CYAC: Student newspapers and periodicals--Fiction. |
Journalism--Fiction. | High schools--Fiction. | Schools--Fiction. |
LCGFT: Novels.
Classification: LCC PZ7.1.L6233 Te 2021 (print) | LCC PZ7.1.L6233 (ebook)
| DDC [Fic]--dc23
LC record available at https://lccn.loc.gov/2021016598
LC ebook record available at https://lccn.loc.gov/2021016599

Book design by Jon Gilbert

Printed in the USA.

9 8 7 6 5 4 3 2 1

for Jerry Chandler

Junkie

We live in a big house, which is good.

I mean, it's not a mansion or anything. It's pretty typical for a house by the lake. Most of the walls have real wood siding, so it's like you're in a cabin. The staircase to the second floor is narrow and so dark it used to scare me when I was little. The only thing that feels big is the living room, with the picture window that looks out on the lake. It's quiet and cozy. But it's big enough that I can almost—almost—get away from the sound of Mom and Dad fighting.

I try to get up early on the weekends, when Dad's home, so I can slip through the living room to the kitchen and eat some Cheerios in peace before the muffled voices start from Mom and Dad's bedroom. It's always Mom first. She's louder. Dad starts out quiet, almost impossible to hear, but then he gets louder and louder.

I don't know what they fight about in the bedroom. In the living room and the car, it's always stuff that needs to be done, stuff that Dad hasn't done because he's away so often.

"The car needs an oil change," Mom might say. "Don't think you're going to sit around all day when that needs doing."

"I'll get to it later," he'll say. "I have yard work to do. And I have some work I brought home that takes priority."

"Your *family* takes priority," Mom will say. "Your wife takes priority. If you were home more often, you could get all these things done."

"I don't understand why you can't do it," he'll say. "You just have to drive to town and get it changed."

"Why can't *you* change it?" she'll say. "You're an engineer and you can't even change the oil in a car. My dad could change oil."

"For the last time, I know how to change the oil. Nobody does that for themselves anymore. It's not 1976. You don't just empty your oil pan and dump it into the lake," he'll say.

And on and on, with the volume going up and up, even though the debate's about some tiny thing. Mom's always the one who turns up the volume. She's always on the attack, and he's always on the defense. If you didn't know them the way I know them, you'd think he was a reasonable person married to a bully.

But I don't mind her acting like a bully so much, because there's more to Dad than meets the eye. He has secrets. I'm pretty sure he's building nuclear bombs or the rockets to put them in. When I was little, he would call from Huntsville every weeknight and read me a bedtime story or make one up. Now that I'm older, he calls around 10:00 p.m., a final item on his checklist before he goes to bed.

And then there's Denise, the name he can't utter in the house. Sometimes he talks about something a "coworker" said or says something about his "staff." But I know he has only one staffer.

There was a time, maybe for more than a year, when Denise would call on weekends, early in the morning. *Duh-neeze*, she

pronounces it. She's American, but she spent part of her childhood in France or Montreal or somewhere, so she pronounces
some words with soft French consonants, as if she had a dip of
Copenhagen in her lip.

"Hi, it's Denize, your dad's assistant," she always says, as if
we've never spoken before. "I can see that he's not there. Sorry
to bodder you."

"You're not bothering. I can get him," I usually say.

"No, please, don't worry," she says. "I'll just text him."

Weird, right? She's in such a hurry to get off the phone.

She's the only person who calls on our landline. Yes, we still
have one, on the wall in the kitchen. With a loud ring. It always
scares me, because I'm usually close to it. The kitchen is my
early-morning place. Mom thinks I'm crazy not to spend more
time in our living room, where there's a big TV and shelves full
of books and a great view of the lake. I can't stand it in there, at
least not when the sun is down. It's like a stage where somebody
passing in the dark could just look right in and see everything
I'm doing. When we watch movies in there, I slump down on
the couch so I can't be seen. When I get up in the morning and
see that Mom left the light on in the living room, I have to go
back upstairs and put my pants on before I can walk through to
the kitchen. Sometimes I walk through with the lights out and
see fishermen on the lake.

"Get over yourself," Mom says. "Nobody's looking at you.
Do you really think you're so attractive that everyone's going to
come around and sneak a peek?"

That's my mom. She won't say it outright, but she's always
getting little digs in about how I'm not attractive. Being attractive is important to her. When I was eight, she put me in a
spring beauty pageant for little girls, where I wore a frilly

dress and sang "God Bless America" in front of a crowd of old people. It was easy to do, a lot easier than you'd expect, because I was sure I was going to win. Dad told me over and over that I was the most beautiful girl in the pageant, and I believed him. But when the pageant was over, I didn't win anything. There were eight girls in the pageant, with one winner and three runners-up. There was a Miss Congeniality award and a Most Talented award. Only two girls, me and a girl who'd gotten poison oak three days earlier, didn't get anything. I was crushed. I wasn't beautiful, which is a tough thing to learn when you're eight.

Dad bought me a plastic tiara and crowned me as "Daddy's princess," which just made it worse. I don't think Mom ever really forgave me. She's convinced, against all evidence to the contrary, that being good looking is an accomplishment you achieve through hard work.

"Beauty is a skill set," she said to me once. "Your dad thinks the pageant thing is a bunch of sexist nonsense, but he doesn't understand. He's not a Southerner. Southern women conquer beauty early so they can move on to other things."

I'm not conquering beauty. I'm not even making an effort. So how could anybody want to peek in the window at me, right?

But I peek in windows. Not in a creepy way. At Christmas, when people leave their curtains open to show off their trees, I read each window closely as we drive by, trying to take in as much detail as I can. Spare, depressing houses where there's a single painting of Jesus on a white wall. Rich, dark-paneled dining rooms with scented candles on the table that you can almost smell. Glimpses of people moving, flashes of the shows on their TVs. I'd sit longer and watch if it weren't such a gross thing to do. It's not that I want to witness a murder or see people having sex. I just want to see what people really do, how they really live. I want to know the truth.

I'm ready, or at least I think I'm ready, for the truth to be bad. Maybe I'll find out I have an illness that will keep me from ever having kids. Maybe I'll get schizophrenia in my twenties, and I'll start hearing voices, and that will be the big challenge of the rest of my life. Maybe when the oil runs out, we'll all start killing one another in some kind of *Lord of the Flies* world. Maybe all men are cheaters at heart, and maybe parents really do love their kids more if they win beauty pageants or basketball championships. I'll be crushed if some of those things are true, but I still want to know. I don't want fake tiaras and hollow assurances that it's okay.

It's hard to know anything for sure in a world that's so fake. Reality TV is fake. My mom spends her evenings watching marathons of shows about "real housewives" who aren't like anyone I know. Teachers are fake: biology teachers who've never done research, English teachers who've never published a word of their own writing.

My whole hometown is fake. Beachside, Alabama, where upper-middle-class Yankees come to build their second homes, with picture windows that face the lake and wooden walkways that meander down to the boathouse at the shore.

Lake Knox-Kilby is fake. It's the biggest fact of life in Beachside. A massive body of freshwater with wooded hilltops jutting out of it. Sportsman's paradise. "At home with the beauty of nature" is how the chamber of commerce presents it. But nothing about it is natural. The lake was created a hundred years ago when Alabama Power created the Knox Dam, filling up miles and miles of mountain hollows with a fake lake. There was once a town down there at the bottom of the lake, called

Lisa, Alabama. I'm named after the town because my mom's family is from there and because my dad likes weird trivia like that. Anyway, the lake made Mom's family rich, or at least it made them not poor. Land on the hillsides suddenly became lakefront property. And decades later, when rich people decided they wanted homes on this lake, Mom's family had something to sell. Mom likes to claim that she retired early because she "sold all the shoreline," though I think other family members did most of the selling.

It's not like I run around pointing a finger at everybody and calling them phonies, like some kind of Holden Caulfield. I get why people go along with fakeness, why they let fakeness slide. Get this: my best friend joined the school newspaper as soon as we started high school. And what's more fake, I ask you, than a school newspaper?

If you've seen one, you know what I'm talking about. Headlines like CHEERLEADERS HOLD CAR WASH TO RAISE FUNDS FOR PROM or VETERANS HONORED IN HOLIDAY PROGRAM. Stuff you already knew or didn't care about, published weeks after the events happened because the paper comes out only three times a year. On the inside pages, editorials about the importance of patriotism or keeping the school bathrooms clean. The only people who read it are the ones whose names are in it—the populars, the club joiners.

In our school paper, there was never the kind of stuff you really want to know about. EVAN MCREATH'S GIRLFRIEND IN VIRGINIA: REAL OR FAKE? Or: CAN TEACHERS SPY ON YOU THROUGH YOUR SCHOOL-ISSUED LAPTOP? Or: STUDENTS SOUND OFF ON BLANKET PUNISHMENTS IN COACH SANDERSON'S CLASS. I guess I could blame the system, but I've always blamed Jamie Scranton, the editor.

Jamie Scranton is one of those Girl Scouts who give the Girls Scouts such a bad name. She raises her hand in class. She collects cans for the Community Food Bank. She volunteers at the animal shelter. Her whole life, apparently, is a series of structured and wholesome activities. I'd love to say that she's a mean, power-hungry Tracy Flick. But no. She's just a Methodist, showing her love of Jesus by doing good deeds in the world. I sat in front of her in social studies last year, and I can confirm that there's nothing dark or evil in there. No secret lust for Dr. Gordon, the world's only semihot vice principal. No pretending to be on her period so she can sneak off to the bathroom and take a pain pill she swiped from her dying grandma. Not even any self-consciousness about her braces, which for some reason are bigger and bulkier than most braces and which instantly transformed her from an oval-faced cutie into a horsey-mouthed librarian type with a slight lisp.

"The doctor says they're stretching my mouth out," she told me once brightly. "Braces don't just fix your teeth. They give you a bigger, better-looking smile."

That's Jamie Scranton. No hidden depths. It's happy, wholesome turtles all the way down. Turtles with braces. How can a well-adjusted, rule-following person like her produce a good newspaper?

"You're being too hard on her," Preethy would always say. "She's a good boss. She treats people well. Why is that a problem?"

That's Preethy Narend, my best friend, the one who used to work for that sad excuse for a paper. I don't hold it against her. She had her reasons. She had her art.

Preethy is the only real artist I know. Manga-style drawings, mostly. She's been into it for as long as I can remember, ever since we were young enough to go to dollar showings of Pokémon movies together at the old Beachside Theater. She's always going on about how much better the world is in anime because the colors are clear and even, the lines bold and simple.

"If I were God," she said once, "I'd make the world over again, just like it is, but everybody would have bigger eyes. It's one change that I know would make everything better, without making anything worse."

"Great," I said. "World War I with big eyes. Serial killers with big eyes. The Donner Party with big eyes."

"Maybe if the eyes were bigger, people would have a harder time killing other people," she said, lifting up the drawing she was working on. "I mean, look. Big eyes make us love something more."

Her entire room is plastered with pictures of eyes. Not photos. Not red eyes, which are gross. Drawings, most of which she did herself, of anime eyes. Eyes like pools of water, reflecting light and color. Eyes with that pinkish thing that's in the corner of your eye, giant and glistening and squishy in the light. I've never had to lie to her about how good they are: they're breathtaking. Sometimes, when she colors them in, they're almost embarrassing to look at in the presence of other people. They seem so personal.

Preethy was the cartoonist for the school newspaper—and she was the only writer besides Jamie Scranton. As long as she wrote enough stories to fill the paper, she got to stay on the staff. And as long as she was on the staff, she got to fill that big box on page 2 with her art. She probably spent more time on those three or four drawings than on all her articles put together. Her first cartoon was, of course, a big eye, with a delicious-looking tear rolling out of it—the caption said something about a mom crying for a daughter killed in a car accident. It ran the same day as Jamie Scranton's editorial on texting and driving. After that, the cartoons got stranger and stranger. Our school mascot is a bear. When Beachside played the Alexandria Valley Cubs at homecoming, Preethy drew a picture of a grown-up bear beating up a dewy-eyed anime-style baby bear. Weird, but everybody seemed to get it. Then there was the one that went with Jamie's editorial on recycling, which had a bunch of woodland creatures weeping over garbage in a creek. If you didn't know Preethy and know why she was drawing these things, you'd think she's a lot more disturbed than she really is.

I guess that could be my fault. I've helped Preethy brainstorm most of her ideas, which I suppose has broken one of Lisa's Key Rules of High School: Don't Get Involved. Extracurricular activities are just another kind of fakeness. Everybody half-assing yearbooks and food drives just to put stuff on their résumés.

"I would think that, as a person of limited attractiveness, you would want to be in lots of clubs in order to meet more people and increase your chances of making friends," Dr. Narend said to me once.

"*Daa-ad*," Preethy replied, hiding her face behind her drawing pad. "Stop. Just stop."

"What did I do this time?" Dr. Narend said. "What, you're worried about 'limited attractiveness'? America is a funny place sometimes. You have to tell everybody they're beautiful all the time or they're so offended. Would it be better if I, an old man, told your young friend she was of unlimited attractiveness? I am an honest man. I tell it like it is."

I'll give that to Dr. Narend. He's not fake, at least not on purpose. He tells it like it is, but I'm not sure he knows what "it" really is. I don't doubt for a moment that he considers himself quite attractive.

"Do thou amend thy life, and I'll amend my face," I told him. Preethy and I picked up a book called *Shakespeare's Insults* at a school bookfair in eighth grade. Nothing but insults from Shakespeare's plays. I'm always looking for a reason to use one.

"You got it backwards," Dr. Narend said. "Falstaff said, 'Do thou amend thy face, and I'll amend my life.'"

It's hard for me to avoid sparring with Dr. Narend, because he's so stunningly sure of himself. But it's just as hard to win. Some people are so smart, even their most oddball decisions seem to work out. Long before Preethy was born, her dad changed his last name to Narend—originally it was Narendra or something similar—because, he insists, Narend is a common English or German surname that would set patients' minds at ease here in Alabama. I ask you: How many Narends do you know, from anywhere? But trust me, you do not want to argue with him about this. He will call in bystanders, even in the middle of a crowded restaurant, and ask them where the name Narend comes from. They'll look uncomfortable—nobody wants to say India because they're not sure what he's getting at—and then they'll say the only right answer, which is Beachside. Dr. Narend's name and face are on three billboards in town.

It's funny how a simple offhand remark—"limited attractiveness"—can hurt more than someone calling you a name right to your face. Mom tells me I read too much into what people say. Once, when I was seven or eight and Mom had friends over for coffee, I packed up my Littlest Pet Shop and marched out of the living room to go play in my own room.

One of her friends said, "Oh, honey, you can play here, we don't mind," but I pretended not to hear her.

"Don't mind Lisa," Mom said as I left. "She's just antisocial."

She probably meant "unsocial." Introverted. Shy. But I went straight to Dad's dictionary and looked up what she'd said. "Antisocial: hostile, menacing, unable to adjust to the laws and customs of society." My life was changed in a moment. I was an enemy of society. Even now I'm half-convinced that's what she actually meant to say.

But it's not like I'm *not* out there trying to meet people, especially boys. For instance, Preethy and I rode the band bus to every away game for almost an entire football season. I'm not into band—when am I going to play the flute in any real-life social situation?—but this year's show was themed "Rainbows," and they needed volunteers to hold up these big rainbow banners in the background during the grand finale. Preethy and I thought it would be a good way to get close to band boys, some of whom are cute and smart, and to sit with them on the bus, which is the place where band members get all their action. It was slow going, though. One trumpet player thought I was a band parent. I thought I was success-fully flirting with the drum major, but then he asked me where I went to school. He'd never noticed me before. And we have homeroom together.

Still, Preethy and I had some pretty good conversations out there on the field, holding the two ends of our banner while the enemy team talked throughout the show. And one of those conversations was what got me into all my trouble.

"I've been meaning to ask you something," Preethy shouted, while the band marched to "Singin' in the Rain."

"I guess I can't stop you," I joked.

"So, Jamie Scranton is running for student body president this year," she said.

"Figures," I shouted.

"And she can't edit the paper and run for office at the same time."

"Shut up!" shouted some parent on the visiting side behind us. A flute solo had just started, and I guess we were talking too loud. When the drums came back in, I picked up the thread again.

"So now you can be editor," I said. "Editor, writer, and cartoonist. It'll be a better paper."

A gust of wind caught the banner, and we both stumbled for a moment.

"Here's the thing," Preethy said. "To be the editor, you have to take Ms. Blandings's journalism class. And I already have chemistry in that period. And you have study hall."

"Me?" I said, a little too loudly, just as the song finished. "Editor of a school newspaper? What's next? Writing an essay about patriotism for the American Legion? Weak."

"But we need someone to be editor," Preethy said. "Without an editor, no paper. Without a paper, no cartoons."

She kept it up later on the band bus.

"I write everything already," she said. "You can be invisible, the way you like to be. Ms. Blandings has already gotten onto Jamie about putting her name in the paper too much. She says an editor should be just a presence in the background. Even the opinion pieces can be unsigned, just like in real newspapers."

"Well, I can't just jump into the class in the middle of the semester like this," I said.

"You can," Preethy said. "Ms. Blandings can get a waiver for you. We've already checked."

"You're plotting behind my back," I said.

I made the mistake of telling Mom about Preethy's pitch on the way home.

"It's about time you did something extracurricular," she said. "And that study hall. It's an embarrassment. A smart girl like you should be in advanced classes for all six periods, like Preethy. No goofing off."

I needed study hall the way Mom needed her morning coffee. Every day, I settled into my desk in the corner, away from the trade school boys and jocks that make up most of the class, and I plowed through my homework. My primary goal every day was to get every scrap of homework done so I never had to think about school after it was over. My secondary goal was to make it through the hour without being sexually harassed. It's amazing, really, how many ways there are for a boy to propose sex to you without making you feel in any way complimented or attractive. I mean, if I said a movie star like Chris Pine or Tom Hiddleston was part of my sexual fantasy life, that would be a great compliment to him. If I had the chance to say it to one of them face-to-face, I'd be the one who felt embarrassed. So why do I feel so icky when Nolan Ramsey, the top some-thingback on the football team, says the same thing to me in front of all his sneering friends?

"I wonder if there are any boys in journalism class?" I said out loud.

Mom beamed.

"That's the spirit," she said. "It's time to get yourself out there and start meeting boys. See? Having an activity will be good for you."

"That's not what I meant," I said. "I want to get away from boys sometimes. If the class were all girls, I'd be fine with it."

Mom kind of groaned. We were getting really close to the elephant in the room that we so often tried to ignore. I'm not her daughter. I mean, I am—I've seen the birth certificate and everything. But I'm not the daughter she wanted. She lives in a house that's like something from *Southern Living*. Seasonal wreaths on the door, antique blue-glass bottles on the bottle tree, a melon baller and a turkey fryer in the kitchen cabinets. She just doesn't have the right family to go with it. A daughter who's half-Yankee, who keeps her hair short and black and wears long sweaters to football games so the opposing team won't stare at her butt. I should be shopping for bright print dresses and hosting outdoor parties for frat bros who semi-ironically wear seersucker to meet your mom. She was okay with Dad when he was gone: it's honorable to leave your family to work for the army, especially if you leave them in a big house. He's a Yankee, though, and that means he's not present even when he's present. He's not a backslapper. He's a man who conveys ideas in sentences rather than rambling stories the way grown men should. I know this was how Mom felt, but she could never say it outright. Pretending your family is perfect is one of the top rules of Southern society. I didn't doubt that, behind my back, she was telling tall tales about how I was Conquering Beauty.

"I don't mean to pry," Mom said. "But I've wondered sometimes if you and Preethy—"

"I'm not dating Preethy," I said, laughing. "We both like boys. Boys who aren't skeevy. That's why we wanted to get onto the band bus. But they're all dating clarinets already."

Mom nodded. "That's how it works," she said. "There are good men out there, like your dad. But they're mostly taken. And when you get one, you have to fight other women off with a stick."

I didn't know what to say. Did she know about Denise? Surely she did; I couldn't be the only one who picked up the phone when Dad's coworker called. Especially since Denise always called the landline, and Mom was the only one who used that phone, stuck in the kitchen because of the cord, chatting with her friends while she arranged magnets on the fridge. (Dad and I like to fit the states together when we can. OCD, I guess; Dad actually threw Texas away because it was too small to fit. Mom always spreads the states out.)

"You're a news junkie anyway," Mom said. "You might as well get into the business."

"News junkie?" I said. "Where are you getting that? I'm your daughter and you don't even know me."

"News junkie," Mom said, matter-of-factly. "What are you always looking at on the internet? You fall asleep with CNN on."

"That's normal," I said. "Just because I'm curious about the world—just because I don't watch reality TV all the time—that doesn't make me a news junkie."

"Yes," Mom said. "Yes, it does. You watch public television, for heaven's sake. What fifteen-year-old watches public television?"

"*Downton Abbey*," I said.

"*NewsHour*," she replied. "You're an old lady in a young woman's clothes. No, you're an old lady with a young woman's body who wears old lady clothes. You should go into the news business because you won't fit anywhere else."

So, a few days later, I got called out of English class to sit down for a job interview with Ms. Blandings, the journalism teacher. It was her planning period.

I liked Ms. Blandings okay. I'd never had her for a class, but

I did think of her as one of the teachers who'd probably be an ally instead of an enemy. She didn't go out of her way to chew out kids who were passing her in the hall just to show that she was in charge. She would just nod hi, like you and she were coworkers. I liked that. It was particularly neat because she was about a head shorter than most seniors, with cute curly short hair and a fresh face that made her look like a student teacher when she was actually, I think, in her thirties. Usually, when a teacher looks like a student, that's the worst. Those are the ones who are always trying to lay down the law.

"So, Lisa," Blandings said, looking at some paperwork from the school office about me. "What newspapers do you read?"

"Well, I guess mostly the *Washington Post* and the *New York Times*, the *LA Times* and the *Chicago Tribune* sometimes," I said. "If you hit the paywall, you can just refresh your browser, and you get another ten articles for free."

"I had no idea you were so interested in journalism," she said.

"I'm not," I said. "I just want to know what's going on in the world."

"So you're interested in public policy."

"I'm afraid of the world," I said. "I want to know what's out there to be afraid of."

"Newspaper editor is a leadership position," Blandings said. "Have you held any sort of leadership position in the past? Band? Sports?"

"Nothing," I said.

"Think outside the box," she said. "You've probably heard Coach Sanderson's take on this. He's always talking about leaders who don't know they're leaders. If you divided the school into cliques, and someone asked you to name your clique and name its leader, who would the leader be? You?"

"No clique," I said. "It's just me and Preethy."

"And who's the leader of that clique?" she asked.

I scoffed a little at the idea of either of us as a leader.

"Well, not Preethy," I said. I don't know why I said it or said it that way, but it was true.

Blandings wrote something down. "Can you tell me the names of two Supreme Court justices?"

I named them all and what side they were on, including the guy who flip-flops sometimes. When Blandings looked at me with a blank stare, I named the only member of the Alabama Supreme Court I could remember.

"How many cabinet members can you name?" she asked.

I got most of them. I mean, who really cares who's secretary of energy?

"Lisa, that's incredibly impressive," she said. "I asked Coach Sanderson the same question two days ago, and he could name only half as many as you did. I don't think most adults know as much about current events as you do."

"This is the second time you've mentioned Coach Sanderson," I said. "You two must talk a lot. Are you in a relationship?"

She actually blushed. She leaned back and moved one hand to cover the fingers of the other hand. Maybe it was because I was looking at her ring finger. Maybe it's because she was thinking about her ring finger.

"If anybody in this school has the skills to work at a newspaper, it's you, Lisa," she said. "Don't let this pass you by."

Strangler

COACH SANDERSON, MS. BLANDINGS TO TIE KNOT.
That was the first headline I wrote for the *Beachside Bulletin* as editor. It went on the back page because it was old news by the time the paper came out. If I accomplished nothing else in my term as editor, I'd coined the term "Blanderson," which stuck fast to the future Ms. Blandings-Sanderson long before she got married and actually changed her name. Preethy got credit for "Blanderson," though. She drew a cartoon with the two of them as anime characters with hearts floating around them, then asked me what the caption should be.

That was the all the fun we were allowed to have with the first issue. Blanderson came down hard on a bunch of other things I proposed to make the paper more fun. Like a gossip page. Or a change to that boring name, the *Beachside Bulletin*. I spent a whole math class ignoring the lesson and brainstorming new names for the paper. A newspaper name should be odd, and it should fall trippingly off the tongue, like the *Modesto Bee* or the *Tallahassee Democrat*.

"The *Beachside Strangler*?" Blanderson said when she saw my top choice. "Surely you can't be serious."

"I'm seriously being ironic," I said. "I'm seriously being edgy. People get their news from a thing called Google. They root for teams called the Indians and the Redskins. You can have an edgy or even totally offensive name and still be taken seriously. And get attention."

Blanderson shook her head. "And what if we actually do have a serial killer in town at some point?" she asked. "What if one of our students or one of our teachers has actually been strangled by a parent or a boyfriend or another kid? You realize that most of the violence in this country is against women? Do you want to make fun of that?"

I didn't say anything. I felt like a little kid who'd gotten caught biting another kid. What could I say? It seemed like a great idea at the time. Now send me to time-out, but don't make me sit here and try to figure out what I was thinking.

"You don't understand the power of the tool that's in your hands," Blanderson said. "The things you say have meaning. You can change someone's name. You've already changed my name just by showing Preethy's cartoon around. Who in the world has the power to change someone's name without asking? A bully, that's who. I took a risk nominating you for this job, you know. Maybe I should have listened to the other teachers."

After that, Blanderson wasn't the same with me. It reminded me of Ms. Guthrie, a teacher we had in middle school. She was fresh out of college, pretty, with neat clothes and a cute fiancé who was a skydiving instructor. Her tests were kind of weird—a lot of us complained that there were always questions about stuff we hadn't gone over in class—but she was warm and friendly and treated us like normal human beings when all the other teachers clearly thought seventh graders were monsters. Then she found out about the Instagram some of the kids had made about all the awkward things she did and said in class. She had to call in a substitute and spent the rest of the day in her car weeping. After that, Ms. Guthrie was a changed woman. All business. Curt and slightly testy, like a mean office lady or a store clerk who doesn't like teenagers. She wasn't unfair or angry, but she had clearly decided she wasn't going to be human anymore.

That's what it was like with Blanderson. Standing in front of the class the next day, she had a fire in her eyes.

"Journalistic ethics," she said. "We covered this the first day, but some of us missed the lesson. Let's talk about the role of the newspaper in the community."

Remember how I said that teachers are all fakes, that science teachers don't do research and English teachers don't write? Well, Blanderson did her best to convince us she wasn't fake. She told us how her dad was a newspaper editor in Mississippi and wrote a history of the civil rights movement that was published by the University of Mississippi Press. She talked about playing with her dolls in the newsroom while her dad worked on election nights. About how newspapers created all the services now provided by the internet before there was an internet—letters to the editor, want ads, dating ads, daily TV listings, sports scores, and stock prices—and how a newspaper could cut a whole group of people out of the community. How Black people were always identified as "Negroes" in old papers, and white women were confined to a "women's page" that was about cooking and clothes and social visits with friends and family.

"Wow," Preethy said when I told her what was going on in journalism class. "Blanderson's on some kind of mission all of a sudden. It makes me wish I was in the class. I wonder what made her so passionate."

I knew what it was. It was me. She wasn't really talking to an entire class about some job most of them would never do. She was talking to me. Blaming me. And it made me mad.

Preethy wasn't any help. She didn't like the *Strangler* idea either.

"As editor, you should ask your staff before you make a big decision like that," she said.

"Well, you and I both know there's not a staff," I said. "There's just you and me."

"Jamie wouldn't put anything in the paper unless she and I agreed on it," Preethy said. "She wanted my opinion on everything. It was tiring, frankly, because half of the decisions were about stuff I didn't even care about."

"Jamie's a manipulative person," I said. "She knows you're an agreeable person, so she knew she could just corral you into doing whatever she wanted."

Preethy kind of huffed, and that was the end of the conversation.

"Blandings keeps talking about 'gatekeepers' and looking right at me," I told Dad that weekend, while we were outside raking leaves. "She's decided I'm this spoiled white girl who's responsible for all the racism and sexism in the media."

Dad said, "Hm," and kept raking for a bit. Then he said: "Well, so what are your plans to write about Black people and their problems? About women's problems?"

"I don't have any plans," I said. "I'm just writing about stuff at school."

He raked a little more before talking again. "It sounds to me like she really trusted you at the start. She respected your knowledge and trusted that you'd take the job seriously. And you violated that trust a little. Just a little, but I've found that once you violate a woman's trust, it takes years to get back to where you started."

That made me mad too. I get so much criticism—about how I look, what I wear, the size of my boobs, and a thousand other things I can't change or don't want to change. None of it hurts like criticism that's right. Dad and Blanderson were right that I'd violated a trust, and both of them seemed to think I really was a spoiled kid or acting like a spoiled kid.

"Denise called this morning," I said. It was a lie.

Dad looked up, a bit surprised. "What did she say specifically?"

I shrugged. "She was just looking for you."

He looked frustrated. "I wish she would stop doing that," he said. "Are you sure there wasn't a specific message?"

He's listening for a code word, I realized. For a moment, I felt a little better about Denise. Maybe all this time, they'd been working on secret national security stuff and passing information about the project in code. But then I realized that a man and his mistress would use code words too. Especially if they worked in a place where secrecy was already part of everyday life.

Not that Dad is very good at keeping secrets usually. By the time I finished putting the rakes away, Dad had already told Mom my whole story.

"Ms. Blandings sounds like a complete bitch," Mom said. "Do you want me to call her and set her straight?"

"No, Mom, I'll deal with it," I said.

"I don't like people being mean to my baby," Mom said.

"You like fighting, and you're looking for a worthy opponent," I said.

"Well, somebody in this family has to be a fighter," she said. "Normally that's the man's role."

Dad just stripped off his work gloves and headed for the laundry room to put them away. It was like he hadn't heard anything.

I used to cry when Mom and Dad fought. I don't know why. When you're the only kid in the house, and your parents are yelling at each other, it's scary. The fights were worse then, when we lived in Florida and Dad came home every day. That's just about all I remember about Florida. I remember the unexpectedly bright spark at the end of a Delta rocket as it lifted over the rooftops and palm trees. I remember crying at the beach because a surprisingly strong wave knocked me over and scared me. And I remember a screaming, birthday-cake-smashing fight that left me pulling used wrapping paper over my head to hide from the world. A clown, in our sandy front yard, dialing his cell phone. Dad standing nearby, trying to convince the clown not to call the police.

As I got older, I changed tactics. When an argument started, I'd pump my fist in the air and say, "Fight! Fight! Fight!" like I was egging on kids at school. I still do that. I don't know why that feels better than crying, but it does.

Here in Beachside, the fights aren't so bad. Dad often tries to sidestep them. I guess you can bear anything for a weekend. Or maybe he does his fighting with Duh-neeze.

"I think your mom is like my dad," Preethy said to me later on the phone. I called her from my room about an hour after I talked to Dad, because for some reason I had started crying.

"Some people like to fight and some people don't," Preethy said. "You know how my dad is. He's always writing letters to the *Birmingham News* to correct something—'Denali' instead of 'Mount Denali,' 'prison' instead of 'jail' or whatever. He's always wanting to lure people into a trap where he can debate them into the ground and show them how smart he is."

"At least your dad knows when to stop," I said.

"He just doesn't know when to not start," Preethy said. "But maybe it's good when somebody says something that prickles people. Maybe it makes them think. I think you've prickled Blanderson, and maybe she's prickling you back."

Later, Dad knocked softly on the door.

"I brought you something," he said. "It's my old Kindle. I wiped it clean, and then I subscribed to the *Columbia Journalism Review* for you. There are back issues in there too. Maybe there's some advice in there about how to approach this."

Dad is smart. How many times a day does someone tell you to look something up, and how annoying does that get? But if you give someone something—a rolled-up newspaper, a flyer, a book—the person's a lot more likely to read it. And so I lay there on my bed, scrolling through the pages on that old-timey gray-and-black screen. I did a search for "high school."

HOW KANSAS HIGH SCHOOL JOURNALISTS
EXPOSED A PRINCIPAL'S PUFFED-UP RÉSUMÉ

REPORTERS ASK: "WOULD YOU LET YOUR SON
PLAY HIGH SCHOOL FOOTBALL?"

THE SUPERINTENDENT'S RACY EMAILS

Whoa. Students had caught a principal lying on her résumé—and gotten her fired. And at another school, the paper was asking if football caused brain damage. And at another school, students had used the state's public records law to get hold of a superintendent's dirty messages. I wanted to do a fist pump after every headline. And then I thought, Why can't we do that here? And then I realized: I'm in charge. I'm the only reason we aren't doing this already.

So I called Blanderson. At home.

"Ms. Blandings," I said, "I've been thinking about what you said. And I want to start over."

Shih Tzu

I want to clear something up right now.

Earlier, Mom said I'm an old lady with a young woman's body who wears old lady clothes. That's not true.

In my mind's eye, I'm that smart girl in class who rocks a mild version of the Goth look, the classic brainy rebel. My hair isn't naturally jet black. You can guess by looking at my parents—Dad has light brown hair with nifty white patches at his temples, like a newscaster. Mom's a redhead slowly turning gray. My hair's naturally mousy brown. You can see that if you look at my roots: a brown stripe down the part in my hair.

In my mental image of myself, I have that goth smoky eye—lashes so thick with kohl, I look like a pirate of the Caribbean—and black nails. But in reality, I usually don't bother. Time spent in front of the mirror is time not spent reading *Anna Karenina* or building that Smurf village on my iPhone. I like to spend my morning imagining I'm in another world, not looking at myself. So it's usually just a few brushes on the lashes with a little bit of mascara and I'm done. No lipstick. I don't have great lips—when we watched *Empire of the*

Sun in history class, one girl told me I looked like the boy in that movie—but the lips I have are plenty red by themselves. So much so that I used to get in trouble at school for wearing makeup when I wasn't.

Realistically, if I did the full-on goth look, I'd have to fight with Mom about it. Just like I fight with her when I'm buying clothes. She has an epithet for everything I pick out. "You'd look like a terrorist." Or "Are you training to be an assassin?" Or the weirdest one: "You look like a hooker from Montreal." Montreal of all places. Has she ever even been to Canada? Where does she get those ideas? And of course the clothes she picks out are really for her imagined daughter, the one with the promise ring, the pink handgun, and the sizable boobs. Clothes that show your putative cleavage and hide everything about your personality.

So that's where the old lady clothes, which are really more like teacher clothes, come from. A compromise between Mom, me, and the dress code. Turtlenecks with long sleeves. Jeans, a simple T-shirt, and a jacket. When I'm on my own, I'll go full goth and bare my pasty white arms for all the world to see. I'll get a bustier and cinch myself into it so tight that boobs and hips are forced to erupt, like flower buds suddenly popping out of a tree in some black-and-white cartoon. Until then, this. It's not how I really look. It's only how I look to Beachside.

Even if I could wear that bustier now, I'm not sure I'd want to share my erupting hips and boobs with this town. I used to think it was strange that guys in trucks were always glaring at us as they drove through intersections, like Mom had made some stupid driving mistake. They never stared at Dad. Finally I realized they were actually staring at Mom, the woman herself. A flash of long red hair and a pale face, and they just had to squint closer to see if the lady at the wheel was hot. There's a lot of ogling that goes on here, a lot of guys who seem about a half second away from unzipping their pants as soon as a teacher's not looking. My old-lady look works as an invisibility cloak for most of these guys. Except for Nolan Ramsey, the jock in study hall who's always making weird jokes about how unsexy I am.

"Are you going to be a teacher as a grown-up?" he'll say. "I always wanted to get with a teacher."

That's why I couldn't believe the news I heard when I went in to make nice with Blanderson.

"I'm glad you want to do real journalism," Blanderson told me, "because now we have a real political race to cover. Jamie Scranton has an opponent for student body president. Nolan Ramsey has thrown his hat into the ring."

I almost fell out of my chair.

"Nolan Ramsey?" I said. "The guy who got sent to the office for saying 'Shih Tzu' over and over again in Family Wellness? How can that be?"

"It's a democracy," Blanderson said. "Anybody can run for anything. We only have one issue of the paper between now and the election. Two if you and Preethy want to work extra hours and put out a special edition. So we need to arrange interviews with them as soon as possible."

"I can't cover this," I said. "I have a conflict of interest. More than one."

Blanderson leaned back and crossed her arms. "Go on."

"One, I have a thing about Jamie Scranton," I said. "She tried to dominate my best friend, my only friend, when she was editor here. You never forget that person who tries to horn in on your friend."

"I don't think you understand what 'conflict of interest' means," Blanderson said.

"Second, I don't like Nolan Ramsey either," I said. "He's always joking, in front of his friends, about how he'd like to have sex with me."

"So what?" Blanderson said. "He's always joking about how he'd like to have sex with me too. Are you having sex with him?"

"Hell no," I said. Blanderson didn't even bat an eye at my "hell."

"Are you having sex with Jamie Scranton? Is either one of them your long-lost half sibling? Cousin?"

I crossed my arms and looked away. "No."

"Do you have some kind of business relationship with either of them?" Blanderson asked.

"No," I said.

"It's probably best that you either like both of them or don't like both of them," she said. "But it really doesn't matter how you feel. You need to get past yourself to do this work. I've never liked the word 'objective,' like you can step outside your body and report on these people from some godlike perspective. But I am asking you to be a bigger Lisa. Someone who can see people as they see themselves. Someone who can question the flaws but who can also present the candidate's strongest case."

I was quiet for a moment.

"You said you wanted to start over," Blanderson said.

"I did," I said. "But is this even important journalism? Isn't this election just a popularity contest? Can the winner really get anything done? I mean, there aren't even parties in these elections. Isn't that what people are really interested in?"

Blanderson leaned forward. "Lisa, those are great questions. I want to make it clear: you can ask them. That's what a newspaper's for—to ask the questions that are on everyone's mind. I'd love to know what the candidates say."

"Even the party question? The principal's always going on about how these things are nonpartisan," I said.

Blanderson shrugged. "School board's a nonpartisan election too. You think people don't ask? You think people don't know? Go ahead and ask."

"Really?" I said.

"Really," she said. "See? This can be fun. This can be real journalism."

"I'll do it," I said. "But I still think there's bigger, more journalistic stuff we could be doing. I've been reading the *Columbia Journalism Review* and looking at what other student papers have been doing. And I've been reading other Alabama papers, and I think I've got an idea."

I pulled out the newspaper clipping I'd saved, from the *Birmingham News.*

MONTGOMERY—Matthew John Houser, convicted of murdering a World War II veteran and his granddaughter in an early 1990s home robbery in Beachside, will die by lethal injection on Jan. 26, the Alabama Supreme Court ruled Friday.

The court rejected Houser's appeal without comment.

"The remaining members of the victims' devastated family have waited 25 years for justice," said Theseus "Teddy" Clayton, lead capital counsel for the Alabama attorney general's office.

"It's time we carried out the sentence the court has imposed," Clayton said.

Houser had just turned 18 when he broke into the Beachside home of Elbert Williams Sr., a retired Beachside resident. Houser believed Williams kept a stash of gold coins in a vault in his basement, apparently because one of Williams' relatives had bragged about the gold.

There was in fact no gold in the house. Houser killed Williams, took $56 from the victim's wallet and left. He also shot and killed 16-year-old Jennifer Williams, granddaughter of Elbert Williams, in the driveway of the Williams home. Prosecutors believe Jennifer Williams arrived at the Williams home just as Houser was leaving and was shot by Houser to eliminate a witness to the crime.

Houser's lawyers never questioned Houser's role in the killing but argued that their client had become delusional after playing role-playing games such as Dungeons & Dragons. The game encourages players to imagine they're raiding underground tunnels full of monsters, in search of gold and silver coins.

That defense stirred a statewide debate about role-playing games, but defense attorneys produced little evidence to support their theory at trial. Jurors rejected Houser's insanity plea and sentenced him to death. Later a new team of lawyers appealed his sentence, making a more conventional plea that Houser suffered from schizophrenia.

Attempts to reach Houser's current lawyers were unsuccessful Friday.

The execution, if it occurs, will be Alabama's first in three years. The state has struggled to maintain supplies of lethal-injection drugs, because of a boycott by European drug manufacturers.

Department of Corrections spokesman Tyburn Riggs said four journalists will be allowed to witness the execution. Under DOC policy, the Associated Press is always allowed a witness. Typically, one seat is reserved for a newspaper in the county where the crime was committed, Riggs said, but Beachside's last daily newspaper folded ten years ago. Three other witnesses—one print reporter and two broadcast journalists—will be chosen at random to view the execution.

I saw Blanderson's eyebrows rise as she read the story.

"This is a big story for a journalist with your experience," Blanderson said. "This seems like an open-and-shut case. You might want to think about what you can do that will really add to what's known."

I knew what she was saying: no.

"Here's what I can add," I said. "I can go to the prison and witness the execution. Look at the last paragraph. There's supposed to be a seat reserved for a newspaper in the county where the crime was committed. We're a newspaper, and we're in that county."

Blanderson lifted her index finger as if she was about to say something. Then she paused and sat for a moment with a troubled look on her face. Then she laughed.

"You know, I really like the idea," she said. "It's bold. It could really make people think—about what a real newspaper is, about why we do executions. If Jamie Scranton had brought me this idea, I would have said yes instantly."

"But not me," I said. "You still don't trust me."

"How would we make our case for this if our paper were called the *Beachside Strangler*?" she said. "I like the fact that you're aggressive. Transgressive. I just want to make sure you're not reckless. Journalism is serious business about serious matters."

"You're just an adviser, right?" I said. "I'm the editor. I can request a seat without your permission. Without your help."

"You can't do it without my permission, because you have my permission," she said. "If you want my help, write up a letter to the appropriate person and run it by me before sending it in. Or go it alone. But you'll find that everybody needs an editor. Even an editor needs an editor. You said you wanted to start over."

I nodded. "I did," I said. "I'll send you the letter when it's done. And I'll set up interviews with the student body president candidates."

"Good," Blanderson said with a smile that seemed human again.

Kitten

The thing Preethy loved most about the newspaper was the fact that it had an actual office. I'm pretty sure it was a broom closet at one point. It was just wide enough to fit a desk at either end, just long enough for the two desk users to work back to back. No windows. The door to the office opened inward, so Preethy couldn't work at her desk unless the door was closed. She and Jamie had created a doorstop—a piece of cardboard wrapped in duct tape—to keep the door from shutting completely, because Preethy had nightmares about being locked in.

The room reeked of Jamie Scranton. An inspirational verse—"I can do all things through Christ who strengthens me"—stood in a small frame near the computer. On the wall, one of those fake inspirational posters: "Get to Work: You Aren't Getting Paid to Believe in the Power of Your Dreams." The famous photo of the kitten hanging by his claws but without any inspirational caption at all. Everything she created, I wanted to add an ironic comment to. Even her irony wasn't ironic enough. It needed another half turn of the screw to be funny. How could she be so smart and not see that?

Blanderson let me out of class to interview both candidates, and I decided to do the interviews in the newspaper office. I regretted that choice as soon as Jamie arrived, hall pass in hand. It was clear that the office was still hers, not mine.

"Sorry there's not a good place to sit," I said.

"I'm used to it," she said. She reached past me to grab the homemade doorstop and expertly slipped it into place before the door shut. Then she turned Preethy's chair around and sat, prim and straight backed. I always wind up slumping when I'm in swivel chairs; there's something stiff and proper in Jamie that I'll probably never have.

"I hope you don't mind if I record the interview," I said. "Blanderson says I'm always supposed to ask first."

"No problem," she said. "No notepad? Just a recording?"

"It feels more like a real conversation that way," I said.

"I find it interesting that so many journalists record," Jamie said. "There's a school of thought that says if you record, it makes you lazy about taking notes. And then one day your recorder doesn't work, and you're left with bad notes and no tape."

"If you don't record, how do you know you got the quotes right?" I said.

"I take pretty skimpy notes," she said. "Just the basics. And then when I hear a quotable quote, I take the time to write it down word for word, and I put a little star by it. And then at the end of the interview, I go back and sort of ask the source about the quotes, like a psychologist. 'So what I hear you saying is this.' That sort of thing."

"You're seeing a psychologist?" I asked.

"Everybody should see a psychologist," she said. "That's why we have school counselors. And don't mind me and all my note-taking stuff. I'm just reminiscing. I'm not trying to tell you how to do your job."

I glanced at the kitten poster on the wall. Somehow I could imagine someone telling the kitten: "I'm not trying to tell you how to do your job." I took a deep breath.

"So let's get started," I said. "Are you a Republican or a Democrat or something else?"

Jamie shook her head. "It's not a partisan election."

"Maybe not, but it's what people want to know," I said. "It's what I want to know."

"If I answer this, it'll affect any future career I might have as a journalist," she said.

"You're running for this job, not that job," I said.

Jamie didn't miss a beat. "Well, I'm a Democrat, of course," she said.

The "of course" really threw me off. This is Alabama. There are Republicans, proud conservative Republicans, and "I'm a Democrat but" Democrats. I'd never heard of an "of course" Democrat.

"Why Democrat?" I asked.

"Because I'm a woman," she said. "Frankly, I don't think the Democrats' track record on women's issues is great. But the Republicans aren't even trying."

Suddenly I found myself liking Jamie. Not because of the party affiliation, but because she was so direct about it. But I knew her likability wouldn't last. I knew at heart she was a yellow-ribbon-wearing, résumé-building booster of clubs.

"What would you do for girls—for young women—at Beachside High to make their lives better?" I asked.

"Honestly, I think we should take a hard look at football," she said. "There's a federal law called Title Nine that says men and women should have equal opportunities in education, including equal opportunities to compete in sports. That's why we have women's volleyball and not men's volleyball. Football is all boys, so we have a completely different sport to create sports opportunity for girls. But everybody knows that in Alabama, nothing is equivalent to football. Whole cities don't shut down so everybody can watch a volleyball game. We don't see a volleyball star and imagine that she'll be living in a mansion one day."

I chuckled. "So the solution is to get rid of football?" I asked.

"If you got rid of football, under Title Nine, you'd have to get rid of volleyball too," she said. "I did think about promoting the idea of women's football, but if we had a team, we'd have no other team to play. But here's something we can do: fairness to volleyball. If the football team has a pep rally every week, the volleyball team should too. We should look at every publication we put out, every poster we put up, and make sure volleyball stars get equal billing. More sports madness for everybody. And it's something a student body president—who has limited powers, really—can actually do."

That actually sounded like a good idea. Bold, feminist, logical. I had to scramble for my next question.

"What would you say to someone who says student elections are all a sham?" I said. "What would you say to someone who says, yes, you really only have limited power, and our votes don't really matter?"

I saw a little flash of anger on Jamie's face as I spoke, just for a split second. She sat up even straighter and stiffer.

"I'd say to that person: You didn't listen to what I just said," she said. "I'd say that maybe you made up your mind about me before you even knew me. I'd say that if you look at me from the outside, I really do look like a person who's just doing 'activities,' but in fact I'm doing what I can do to make the world a better place. I'd say that playing the rebel and criticizing everything is more about ego than it is about getting things done. And I'd say that as a woman, I don't have much chance of winning that ego game anyhow. It's made by men, for men."

I was quiet for a moment. Suddenly I wished I had a notebook. Something to hide behind as I frantically scribbled down Jamie's quote and put a star beside it.

Jamie leaned in.

"If you don't mind my asking," she said, "who is it that's saying these elections are all a sham? Who's really asking this question?"

Twenty-five minutes later, Nolan Ramsey knocked on my office door. I realized too late—right when I heard him tapping—that maybe it wasn't such a good idea to meet up, alone, with a guy who had basically sexually harassed me all year. I picked up a big legal pad and a pen, holding them in front of me almost like a shield for a moment, then opened the door.

It wasn't quite the Nolan Ramsey I'd expected. Yes, he was in his letterman jacket as always, muscular and tanned with a mop of surfer-boy bleach-blond hair. It was like he couldn't decide whether to be a rock-star type or a muscle-bound jock, so he'd gone for both looks at once. He would have been better looking if he'd picked just one.

What was new was this: he was shorter than me. I guess that was always the case, but I didn't notice until he edged past me to get to Preethy's chair. He was smaller than usual, too, in some other way. He had a cowed look, like a kid called in for a talk with the principal. He was scared of this interview or scared of me. Or maybe this was just who he was when he wasn't surrounded by a crowd of teammates.

I felt a weird urge to put him at ease. But I was uneasy too.

"Just so you know, I'm going to record the interview," I said. "Just to make sure I get it right."

"Fine," he said, flopping down into the chair and setting his backpack on the floor. "I just hope I don't screw this up."

Uncomfortable quiet as I started the recorder.

"Okay, let's leap right in," I said. "Are you a Republican, a Democrat, or other?"

"Whoa," he said. "Was I supposed to fill something out about that? I didn't realize that was part of running for SGA."

"No, it's just something I'd like to know because I think the readers would like to know," I said. "So what are you?"

He kind of snorted a little laugh.

"A Republican," he said. "Of course. It's Alabama. I thought we were all Republicans. Isn't Jamie Scranton a Republican?"

"I guess what I'm trying to get at is, *Why* are you a Republican?" I said.

"Well, I love America," he said. "I want a strong military. My grandfather was in Vietnam, and his dad was in World War II."

"So, what will you do for Beachside High to make things better for students?" I said.

"Well, I love America," he said again. "I love Beachside and I love Beachside High. I'm not going to pretend I know a lot about student government and how it works, but I can figure it out. The important thing is to elect somebody who's proud of the school and who the school can be proud of."

"So why should I vote for you over Jamie Scranton?" I said.

"I'm not really running against Jamie," he said. "If she wins, she'll do a fine job. I'm just giving people a choice. They can look at her and look at me—two great candidates—and decide for themselves who they like best."

"You make it sound like just a popularity contest," I said.

He shrugged and smiled.

"Is that all this is?" I asked. "Just a popularity contest?"

He sat up a little straighter. "Um, maybe you think so, but I don't," he said. "What about you? Are you a Republican or a Democrat?"

Ah, so it was on. But I'd come prepared.

"I shouldn't say," I said. "But I can honestly say I'm not either. Or any other party. I dislike all the parties equally."

"Communist is a party," he said. "You dislike Republicans and Communists equally?"

"Okay, maybe not equally, but in complicated ways," I said. "But this interview's about you and not me."

"Well," Nolan said, "you're kind of making me uncomfortable. You're asking all kinds of things about party, which isn't part of this race, and I don't know where you're coming from. I kind of feel attacked a little bit."

"A lot of people feel attacked at school every day," I said. "As student body president, what do you intend to do about bullying?"

Nolan cocked his head and narrowed his eyes.

"Look, let's talk about something," he said. "You and me. Turn that recorder off."

"Why?" I said.

"Off the record," he said. "Isn't that something real reporters do? Just two people talking for a minute. So we can maybe start over again."

I wanted to say, *I am a real reporter.* But I turned off the recorder. And Nolan's face softened again with that puppy-dog look he'd had when he first entered the room.

"I do want you to know I'm sorry about some of the things I said in study hall," he said. "I know you probably think I was joking and making fun of you. But I really am attracted to you. That was real."

Whoa. Not what I expected to hear.

"So why didn't you do the things a guy does when he's attracted to a girl?" I said. "Like actually ask me out? Try to sit with me at lunch? Invite me to the homecoming dance?"

Nolan shrugged.

"I don't know," he said. "It's hard when I'm with the other guys. It's hard to say what I mean. It's hard to know what I mean."

"So you didn't mean that you looked at my yearbook photo while you—"

"Here's what I mean now," he said. "And this is real. Go out with me. I'm asking now. Let's start over again. Go to the movies with me."

I wish I could describe what I felt at that moment. Nolan wasn't unhandsome. And there he was, sitting in front of me and acting like a decent, articulate human being for the first time. Asking me out. There was that, plus the fact of the public Nolan who'd made me feel so bad in study hall. A Nolan I knew would be back as soon as we stepped into a room with other people. And then there was another fact that was more important than both of those things.

"I can't date you," I said. "I'm the editor of the school newspaper, and you're running for office. It's a conflict of interest."

"What?" he said. I could see the two Nolans in his response. Good Nolan was genuinely hurt that I'd rejected him. Good Nolan had thought a moment of sincerity would win the day. And Bad Nolan, study-hall Nolan, couldn't believe that mousy little Lisa had turned him down. Bad Nolan was indignant.

"A conflict of interest?" Nolan asked. "Really? Lisa, it's just a school newspaper. Nobody really cares."

"I care," I said. And then, just then, I realized I really did care. I cared about that newspaper the way I'd never cared about anything at school before.

Nolan scooped up his backpack but didn't get up. He sat there for a moment with his hand over his heart, like I'd punched him there.

"This is why I act the way I do in study hall," he said. "This is why guys act the way we do. Because we're always the ones who have to ask. And then we get rejected, and it hurts, and we're supposed to just tough it out and ask somebody else. Nobody cares when our hearts get hurt. We're not supposed to have hearts."

"You didn't ask," I said. "You ordered. 'Go out with me.'"

"I was being self-confident! Girls are supposed to like that!" he said. "Look, please. I am asking you. Because I do like you. I like you a lot. Will you go out with me?"

I threw my hands up. "Conflict of interest," I said. "I can't, no matter what I want."

"This is bull," he said, standing so suddenly it kind of scared me. "How are you not conflicted already? You're breaking my heart. You want to date me. Even if you don't date me, you have a conflict. This conflict."

"I don't want to date you," I said. "And I'm sorry about your heart. Really. I appreciate your being honest with me."

I really did feel sorry for him. As for not wanting to date him, I don't know if I was lying or not. I felt like I'd just met an actor who played a villain on TV but was warm and friendly in person. Date you? I don't know you.

"None of this better wind up in the paper," he said, and stormed out.

"Are you sure you want to create a real newspaper?" Preethy asked later. "You could have a fake newspaper and a pretty okay boyfriend. No one expects a real newspaper, no one but you. No one would mind."

On the phone the next night, I told the whole thing to Dad. I guess I didn't give him all the details of the things Nolan had said to me in study hall—he would have gone through the roof—but I gave him the basics.

"It seems to me that if you weren't producing a real newspaper, you wouldn't have had this moment," he said. "You're forcing people to be honest about things. And now you know that some of your classmates are more human than they let on. And you know some things about yourself that you didn't know. Sounds to me like you're better off sticking to newspapers than chasing boys. Who knows what you'll uncover next?"

He was right. I knew it as soon as he said it. And then something flipped in my gut. I knew that there were some things I wanted Dad to be more honest about too.

"Dad," I began. I wanted to say, Tell me the truth about Denise. But I just couldn't get it out. Maybe even journalists have a limit on how much truth they can take in each day.

Clown

The next day I got a pass out of journalism class, supposedly to work on my story about Jamie and Nolan and the student body president race. I got set up in my closet office with my mostly blank notepad at my left hand, my recorder at my right, and a blank screen in front of me. And I spent the next thirty minutes watching funny videos of college boys playing *Funkirk 2*.

Yes, that *Funkirk*. The video game that's at the heart of everything that's wrong with the world right now.

It's a sick idea on a number of levels—I mean, a multiplayer game where superpowered clowns fight in key battles and military campaigns of history, from Waterloo to the Tet Offensive. And yes, it's riveting. I mean, the battle maps are so realistic, it's almost like you're there. And there's the sick humor of it, like when farting noises give away some clown's position and he gets blown into meaty bits. And then there are the boys who play the game and post videos, with commentary, on the internet. Some of them are actually kind of harmless and funny, but most are sick in some way, growling about bitches and rape or claiming this is serious training for their future careers killing people for their country. *Funkirk* is pretty much a country club for neo-Nazis, and yet people treat it like it's *Pac-Man*. Every boy I know plays it, and half the girls too.

I'm addicted too, not to the games but to the culture war over it. If you post a link to the latest *Funkirk*-video outrage on social media, you can bet I'll watch it. And after I'm done I'll post a response shaming the boy who made the clip. And then I'll watch and comment on another clip. And another. Until I feel like burned out, like a foreign correspondent covering an imaginary war.

"Jeez, Lisa," I said to myself. "What are you doing? You're supposed to be writing."

I know now exactly what I was doing. Did you know that avoiding writing is half of the writing process? That's how it works for me. When I've got my notes, when the images are still fresh in my mind, when I have two hours to turn the thing in, that's when I start playing *Candy Crush* like an old lady.

I turned off the *Funkirk* videos, looked up a phone number on a state website, and dialed. Video games weren't the only distraction available to me.

"Alabama Department of Corrections," a woman's voice said. "How may I direct your call?"

"If I wanted to witness an execution, how would I go about doing that?" I said.

"Are you a member of the victim's family? Inmate's family?"

"I'm with the media," I said.

"Hold on a minute," she said, noticeably colder.

On hold, I listened to a recording of a growly voiced guy—I imagined him wearing a drill-instructor hat—flatly reading out instructions about how to contact inmates, what you can't bring on prison visits, and so on.

"Tyburn Riggs, communications," said a voice.

"Mr. Riggs, I'm the editor of the *Beachside Bulletin*," I said. "I'm trying to get a seat to cover the Houser execution. Did you get my letter?"

"Mmmm," Riggs said. "Give me a moment. I'll pull it up. Aha. *Beachside Bulletin*. That's a high school newspaper?"

"Beachside High School," I said.

"And you're the faculty advisor?" Riggs asked. "Your student is the one who sent this letter?"

"I'm the editor of the paper," I said. "I sent the letter."

Riggs exhaled. A sigh, I guess, but a little angrier than a sigh.

"Look, miss, I'm not sure we can help you with this request," he said. "Our rules require a seat for a real newspaper—"

"This is a real newspaper," I said.

"Under state law, a real newspaper is a newspaper of general circulation," he said. "Do you have subscribers? Do you have delivery drivers? Do you run legal ads?"

"What are legal ads?" I asked.

"See, this is why I'm quite sure you're not a newspaper according to state law," he said. "Legal ads are announcements from the state, about upcoming bills and so on, that according to state law have to be advertised in newspapers. It's been that way since the 1800s, something the legislature did to make sure people know what their government's doing. Legal ads are just about the only revenue some papers have these days. If you were running a true, adult-world newspaper, you'd know that."

True newspaper! We'll see about that.

"Will *Birmingham Buzz* be able to get a seat at the execution?" I asked. "Are they a real newspaper? Do they run legal ads?"

"Birmingham Buzz is the biggest print media organization

in the state," Riggs said. "It's the owner of several of the oldest newspapers in the state."

"They bought up a bunch of small-town papers so they could shut them down," I said. "They replaced them with a statewide magazine and a website that posts football news and pictures of girls on spring break. Do they run legal ads?"

"They do still publish all the papers you're talking about, twice a week," he said. "And I believe they do run legal ads."

I guess it's all a matter of how you define things. In gas stations in small towns all over the state, you can find *Buzz* papers for sale at the counter. Every one of them has a local name—*Demopolis Buzz* or whatever—but it's the same content you get in Birmingham. Were there legal ads in each of these papers? I'd never looked.

"You believe they run legal ads," I said. "Do you know?"

"I know that the owner of several well-known print newspapers has a claim to be a newspaper of general circulation, and the *Beachside Bulletin* does not," Riggs said. "And I have to say I really don't understand why a girl in high school would want to witness an execution anyway. Does your principal know you're doing this?"

I should have known, right then, what was coming next.

Cake Smasher

The next morning, I had trouble getting out of bed. It had been one of those autumn nights when the air gets surprisingly cold. My eyes popped open at about two or three minutes before five, as they always do, and for a moment I had this feeling that I was in a sleeping bag in a tent with a dewy coldness outside and warm snuggliness inside. I closed my eyes and pretended for a while that I was camping, the way I did during my brief career in the Girl Scouts, before the "God and my country" fiasco. I was happy just then, in those three minutes before the alarm went off. Is it just me, or is a bed on a cold morning the closest thing to paradise?

Downstairs in the picture window the lake was a mirror, reflecting the dark blue of the night sky back up at itself. Emptiness looking at emptiness. Sometimes the water is so calm it's not like water at all but like some thicker fluid, maybe motor oil in a pan. No boats were on the lake just then, so I stood wrapped in my quilt and watched for a bit. Then to the kitchen.

Mom and Dad's laptop was on the kitchen table, open, with a screen saver dancing around. Time to check the news. I touched the mouse pad and was blinded by the sudden white and blue of a Facebook page.

Denise Fabron's Facebook page.

There she was, my dad's mysterious coworker. Partner in, well, crime. Her profile picture was of her at a blackboard teaching about some sort of equation, with a serious look and her long hair up in a bun. That must have been some time ago. Her latest posts had her with short hair, shaved on one side. She seemed to think that was her best side, because she posted selfie after selfie where her long kissable neck and three earrings were at the center of the shot. Around the neck whirled a galaxy of excitement. Sometimes the neck was sitting down to a great meal at a brewpub. Sometimes it was at colorful Alabama locations, Dreamland Bar-B-Que or the Trash Pandas' stadium. A demure boyfriend appeared in the periphery of some of the shots. Maybe an inch shorter than her, with a fit body, close-cropped hair, and a well-trimmed beard. A boyfriend. I tried to read her posts, but almost all of them were reposted headlines from French newspapers about figure skating, Nutella, and physics.

And then I realized: there was a little red circle on "Messenger." I clicked on it: "You have a message from Denise Fabron."

My hand shook. Do I read it? Do I want to know, for sure, why Dad was creeping on his coworker in the middle of the night? I could click and see a bunch of work-related stuff that would set my mind at ease. Or I could click and read something that would rip my world to shreds. Smashed birthday cakes and clowns calling the cops. And maybe I'd be the cake smasher this time.

And then, out of nowhere, a FaceTime call. Suddenly I'm

looking at my own early-morning face on camera, with the name "Denise Fabron" at the bottom of the screen.

Before there were cameras everywhere, did people know this feeling? I was mad that someone could prod me with a request for an interview there in my kitchen while I was in my underwear. Guilty that I'd been caught, in a way, creeping on someone else's creeping. Mad. Just mad at everything. I slapped the laptop shut. Then opened it again and held the Power button until it shut down. I didn't want the chaos that would ensue if Mom saw Denise's Facebook message, whatever it was.

I went back to the picture window, wrapped in my quilt. Some houses had lights on now, with tempting signs of movement in the kitchens. The sky was a slightly brighter blue. A fishing boat was on the water now, with no light on, drifting. I didn't care about being seen by a fishing guy just then. I didn't care about much of anything. What was wrong with people that they always had to have too much? Why did someone have to have a beautiful neck and a boyfriend and my dad too? Why did everybody want to be a cheater and a dad, a creep and a student body president? What was wrong with me that I didn't want to conquer beauty so I could get on Facebook and show my neck and my shoulders and make people jealous?

"What's gotten into you?" Preethy said in homeroom later that morning. "You finished your stories about the student body presidential race. We print the paper tonight. You should be happy. Your name in print."

Just then, Preethy seemed so much younger than me. So untroubled.

"I guess I kind of went to a dark place this morning," I said. "There's a lot going on at home. No, there's nothing going on. Nothing new. I'm just seeing what's going on a little better."

"Do you want to talk about it?" Preethy said. "Come over to my place ton—"

Just then, the intercom barked. And it called my name. *"Please report to Dr. Gordon's office."*

An "ooooh" went up from the homeroom crowd. Dr. Gordon's the vice principal, at the top of the discipline chain. He walks the halls with his salt-and-pepper hair and his American flag lapel pin and his white legal pad, attached to an aluminum clipboard, on which he writes down all the world's sins. There's only one reason to go to Dr. Gordon's office, and that's because you're in trouble. If your grandmother dies or your big sister's in a car wreck, the principal comes down and pulls you out of class personally.

I couldn't think of anything I'd done wrong, but it's funny how you can find something to feel guilty about if you just look. In the last few weeks, I'd actually broken fewer rules than usual because I'd been so busy with the paper. The only odd thing I'd done recently was spy on my dad's coworker on Facebook and stand in front of the picture window with a blanket around me. As I climbed the stairs to the office, I had a sudden frightening thought that maybe I'd actually accidentally taken that FaceTime call and had exposed myself in some way on camera. Or that somebody had seen me in the picture window and thought I was a flasher or something. A stupid idea, I know. I mean, I was in my own house in a blanket. If anything, the person looking in should have been in trouble.

It didn't help that when I arrived at the office, I could hear Gordon, behind the door, talking about "this kind of exposure." I knocked lightly and then just barged right in, ready to get it over with.

Blanderson was there. And Gordon, looking exasperated, almost as if he was about to cry.

"Lisa," he said. "Have a seat."

I did, and everything was quiet for a moment. Gordon looked up at the ceiling with a sigh, trying to figure out what to say.

"Lisa," he said. "I don't know you that well, but you seem like a nice girl. Smart, well adjusted, from a good family. At your age, most girls are learning to drive and finding a boyfriend, and I just wish you could explain to me why you would do something like this."

Oh, God, I thought. It *is* that.

"How did you find out?" I said.

"Tyburn Riggs from the Department of Corrections called me," he said. "He told me everything."

I couldn't stop myself from bursting out in laughter. "Oh, that!" I said. "That's what this is about."

"Now, look, Lisa, I'm all for free speech," Gordon said, in the way people say it when they're not all for free speech. "The press is important. But there has to be some decency. Why would you want to go see someone get put to death? Why would you want to do something ghoulish like that?"

"Um, because our state government is doing it, and they invited reporters to cover it?" I said. Then, more confidently: "Come to think of it, because our taxes are paying somebody to do this. Because it's being done in our name."

Blanderson stuck out her hand, indicating me.

"See?" she said to Gordon. I wasn't sure what that meant. Did she have my back or not?

"Yes, but why you?" Gordon said to me. "Why does it have to be a school newspaper? Can't someone else cover this story? That's how you journalists say it, right? Cover the story. Why can't a real newspaper do it?"

"There's not—" Blanderson and I started at the same time.

"You go," I said.

She nodded. "There's not a newspaper in the entire county, not a 'real newspaper' of the sort you're describing," she said. "There literally isn't anyone else from Beachside—the location of the murders—who can get in, at least as a reporter."

Gordon sort of frantically moved papers around on his desk. "But the reaction in the community is going to be . . . I just don't get it. Why does anybody need to see this thing being done?"

"That's a question you should ask the state," I said. "Why do they invite people to come out? Why do they publish the last meal and all?"

"That's a question we ought to ask, Lisa, in our story on this," Blanderson said.

"There's not going to be a story on this," Gordon said.

"That's for Lisa to decide," Blanderson said.

"That's not what the courts say," Gordon said. "The courts say we have authority to review—"

"Let me stop you right there, Mark," Blanderson said. "We can go back to court if you want to and see if they still feel that way. We can go there. Or I can go to the teachers' association and see what they think about what's going on here."

Wow. Props to Blanderson.

Gordon turned to me, with the pained look again

"Lisa, I hope I can convince you to see this from my perspective," he said. "I want every child at this school to feel like this is a welcoming place for them, even if they don't feel welcome at home. What if there's a child at this school who's related to the victim? Or to the man being executed?"

"Well, cool then," I said. Blanderson and Gordon both winced in disgust. "I mean, not *cool* cool. But that would be a great reason for us to cover this story. Because one of our readers is directly affected. It's all the more reason for us to look at it and not keep it a secret."

I could tell then that Gordon was done talking to me, maybe forever. He turned to Blanderson.

"I think you see what the problem is here," he said. "You need to handle it."

Blanderson escorted me to first period—a walking, talking hall pass. Except she wasn't talking much. She was scary quiet, in fact.

"That's the first time I've been called to the office," I said. "It's not what I expected. I thought it would be like 'You don't have free speech, young lady,' but instead he was acting like I was about to stab him. Manipulating my emotions. That's how you control people."

"Hm," Blanderson said. Nothing else.

"You were a badass in there," I said. "Badass" is a banned word at school, but I've never known a teacher to complain when it's applied to her. "You're like, 'Lisa has rights and I have rights, and I'll see you in court.' Bad*ass*."

Blanderson stopped in her tracks. Just staring at the floor with her hands stretched out a little, like she was trying to stop herself from blurting out something mean.

"What?" I said. "You agree with him?"

She regained her composure and looked at me.

"Lisa," she said. "I want you to think for a moment about what he said. About a kid who could be going to this school, who could be reading—in one way or another—about the death of a family member in our paper. That's not a reason not to tell the story. But it is a reason to think very hard about how we approach it. So many kids come into my class thinking reporters are ghouls, that they're crass and bloodthirsty. Being like that is not our job. Sometimes our job is to be more human than the circumstances. It's always our job to be more human than we absolutely have to be. Just because the state puts this on display and just because we have a right to see it doesn't mean there's no point in taking care.

"I'll tell you a story my dad told me once," she continued. "He had to cover a fatal wreck on a rural highway in the middle of the night. Sometimes, as a reporter, you arrive early enough to see the bodies before they're in the ambulance. And that's what he saw. A truck driver was lying on the road, his body literally cut in half. A state trooper told him the trucker was still alive when troopers found him—still conscious, somehow. The trucker talked to the trooper. He mentioned his wife and his kids, all by name, and gave him a message for each one. The trooper wrote them all down.

"And those last words, or a paraphrase of them, wound up in the paper," Blanderson continued. "My dad wrote a heart-rending story about the family man who died late at night, missing his kids. He got quotes from other truckers at the company, who talked about how the trucker loved fishing with his daughter and surprising his wife with presents. The one thing that wasn't in the story was that one image. The image of the man lying on the road, cut in half and still alive. That image haunted my dad for the rest of his life. Sometimes, years later, I'd catch him in a dark mood or even crying, and he'd tell me it was because of that. But he never told anyone but me. This is what journalists do. You're not there to cover the gore and the severed limbs and all that. You're there to take the broken bodies and put them back together. To turn a corpse into a human again one last time, to let no one die as an unnamed person in a police report."

Damn. What to say to all that?

"I . . . I'm not sure I can do that," I said.

"I believe in you, Lisa," she said. "But sometimes you do make me wonder if you really *can* do that. *Beachside Strangler*? 'Cool'? I'd like to be able to tell Dr. Gordon he shouldn't worry about you, but sometimes I'm not sure myself. I'm still not sure you understand the power that's in your hands."

I crossed my arms and just stared at her for a bit.

"I'll tell you what I don't understand," I said. "I don't understand why you don't believe in me. We had this talk. The *Beachside Strangler* talk. And I agreed with you. Why are you still on my back?"

Blanderson rolled her eyes. "Gifted kids," she said. "They're all alike. Do you think that because we had a talk and you understood what I said—up here in your head—that it's a lesson learned, a grade in the grade book, done and done? Journalism is a *discipline*. A discipline is about learning the same thing over and over because there's more to it than understanding it up here. You've got to understand it *in here*." As she said this, she touched not her own chest but mine, in what I can only describe as a fist bump to my heart.

"Okay," I said. "Okay, sensei. I mean it. You're the master. I'm the apprentice. I'm bowing to your wisdom. What can I do to get this knowledge *in here*? What's next?"

"Here's what I think," she said. "I think the next time Gordon asks about families—families of the victim or families of the shooter—we should be able to answer him. If they're here, we should know who they are. We should talk to them. They're our story. People are our story."

"How do I do that?" I asked.

"I'd start with yearbooks," she said. "The school library's full of them."

Later that day, Blanderson gave me a pass to the library, where I sat with a big stack of Beachside High yearbooks. I was supposed to start with this year and work my way back, searching for Housers and Williamses—kids related to the murderer and the victims. But I couldn't resist going straight to the 1980s and looking for Matthew Houser and Jennifer Williams first.

Man, the eighties. People get on *me* for dressing like an old lady, but you should look at some of those photos. Look past the big hair that everybody talks about. Here's a boy who's maybe sixteen, in square wire-rimmed glasses, a short-sleeve Oxford shirt, and a *tie*. On the facing page, there's a more handsome dude with clear skin, fit but not bulky, the kind of kid who looks like he'd be on the tennis team at a private school. No glasses, but he's got a skinny white tie against some kind of colored shirt with a *sport coat* over it. Kids dressing like bankers and grocery store managers.

Houser wasn't like that. He wasn't hard to find—one of the few kids wearing a T-shirt in his photo. Thin embarrassing moustache, dark hair in kind of a butt cut. For some reason, his face in the shot was much bigger than everyone else's on the page. Maybe they cropped the shot closer to hide whatever was printed on his T-shirt. Maybe there were instructions to come dressed up for photos, and he didn't listen, or didn't have dress clothes, or maybe didn't even have someone to buy them for him. The way he leaned in, his lack of a smile, made him look like he was trying to put on an air of rebellious toxic masculinity. But his eyes, man. They looked worried, scared. I don't know how to describe it. He looked like he'd seen something that had unnerved him. Not something that had really happened, like, in front of him, but something inside himself. His eyes looked the way I feel about half the time.

I found Jennifer Williams a couple of grades down. Actually, two girls with the same name. Jennie Williams was a tall, healthy-looking girl with braces that were easy to see because she had this big, open smile. She wore a bright printed blouse that I knew was supposed to be formal, but it looked a bit like a Hawaiian shirt to me. I felt like I knew her just from the photo—athletic and boy crazy and willing to take a dare. Popular with the boys, nonthreatening to other girls. But somehow I also knew that this wasn't the Williams I was looking for. Next to her, a girl with hair permed into a kind of topiary, white dress with puffy shoulders and three big buttons down the front. I could imagine her arguing with her mom, saying it looked like a clown suit. Her smile was a kind, forbearing smile. Her eyes smiled too, and I guess they were brown, because in the photo they looked like two little beads. She seemed like someone who was waiting to have her say. In that clown suit, next to a more popular girl who had stolen her very common name, Jennifer Williams was just waiting and observing the scene, thinking witty Jane Austen thoughts about what she saw and waiting to leave this town and put all her wisdom to use in another life. Or maybe she'd stay here, marry some louder man, and keep her Mona Lisa thoughts to herself forever, in Beachside but never really in Beachside.

Except she wouldn't do either of those things. She wasn't in the next year's yearbook. Neither was Houser.

I guess I shouldn't have been shocked by what I noticed next, but I was. There on the yearbook page, not far from where Jennifer Williams would have been, was Mom. Maiden name: Woodley. Like all the girls on the page, she had her hair in a perm, though someone had gotten her perm right—not too big, not too flat, natural looking. Clear skin, big eyes, big square metal earrings, shoulder pads, yes, but under a soft, feminine cardigan-sweater kind of thing. Conquering beauty. I don't know why it never occurred to me that Mom had been there the whole time, sitting in the same classrooms with Williams and Houser, standing in the lunch line, maybe working the same Bunsen burners in the lab.

"Jennifer Williams," Mom said later, as we were cooking dinner. "Which one?"

"You know which one," I said.

"Her," Mom said, turning to look in the fridge. "Yeah, well, it's sad. I didn't really know her. And then after the thing happened, everybody knew her. I don't just mean that everybody knew her name. I mean, all of a sudden, there were reporters everywhere, and so many people turned up saying they were her best friend and they were so broken up about it, when you knew they really hadn't been close to her. And then after about a week, they were all gone. The reporters. And we just went back to school, and everything was like normal. It happened over the summer, you know."

"And people just forgot about it?" I asked. "There wasn't an assembly or something?"

Mom shrugged.

"It happened over the summer," she said. "We didn't hold assemblies like that back then. Maybe if a kid died during the school year. Maybe if it was the head cheerleader and she died over the summer. Helping people to cope wasn't much of a thing back then. There was a kid who sat behind me in homeroom in seventh grade. Daniel. Polite, smart, not all that cute but pleasant. He didn't say a lot of those ignorant things that boys say so often. I liked him. And over the summer, he choked to death on a chicken bone. It was in the paper. Not a word about it when we went back to school in the fall. If you needed to cope, you should have done it by then."

I shook my head. I hate those assemblies, and I'm with Mom on people who wail over tragedies that aren't all that connected to them. But to ignore a death just seemed cold. If I choked on a chicken bone, would there be anybody at school to mourn me? Just Preethy, consoled by her new bestie, Jamie Scranton?

"What about Houser?" I asked. "Did you know him?"

"Back then, people like me didn't really even go to school with people like him," she said. "There were classes for people who were going to college, and for girls who weren't going to college, there were, like, typing classes or something, and then the boys on the trade-school track went to homeroom, then got back on the bus and spent their whole day at trade school. So he must have been in trade school, and she must have been on the typing track."

"So all you know about this is that a trade-school boy killed a typing-class girl," I said.

"And that's all I need to know," she said. "I'm not a cop. The cops did their jobs. Remember, I used to sell real estate. I sold Beachside. It's better if I can look people in the eye and say, 'I don't know a lot about that.' Why are you asking about it, anyway?"

It was the first time in a while that I'd seen Mom in "I sell Beachside" mode. You could count on her to forget everything that didn't fit her Theory of Beachside, in which crime is low and natural beauty is everywhere.

"Please tell me this is not something you're going to write about in the school paper," Mom said.

I just walked away, out onto the porch, as if I hadn't heard what she'd said. Mom is a such a fighter, you have to really be on your game to take her on by yourself. Go ahead and call me a sullen teen, but sometimes running away is the best course of action.

Running away, out into nature. The sun had just set, and the lake was clear and dark blue. I thought of all those stories down there below the water. Fortunes lost. Gravestones no one had seen in a century. Homes and stores and churches still rotting, down where the sunlight was so dim only a catfish could see.

Blond

Ever had someone to tell you not to be so sensitive? That you're just looking for things to worry about? I get that all the time. And I'm not buying it. Usually when my spider-sense is tingling, there's something creepy going on.

And that's how it was the next morning at school. As soon as I walked in the door, passing kids from other grades I didn't even know, I was aware that people were looking at me. Not giggling or pointing, just watching to see what I'd do next. Looking up as I passed, then looking away as I noticed them looking. I felt a bit like I felt when Preethy and I were on the football field, holding up banners.

As I turned down the hallway toward my locker, I got a sense of why people were staring at me. The hallway was covered with a new set of posters. On white poster paper, a familiar elephant figure drawn in blue and red marker.

RAMSEY. GOP. FOR THE WIN, read one.

REAGAN. RAMSEY. REPUBLICANS, said another. And another: MAKE BEACHSIDE GREAT AGAIN.

If I ever felt any hint of attraction to Nolan Ramsey, it was just then. These were good ads. Simple and smart. Bold images and big friendly letters. I knew none of Nolan's friends were smart enough to come up with this. There was a smart boy inside Nolan who could be attractive if he'd just get his head out of his ass.

Preethy, as usual, was at her locker, right next to mine. And standing there with her, where I was supposed to be, was Jamie Scranton.

"Hey, Lisa," Preethy said with a defeated tone that suggested she wasn't looking forward to the coming conversation.

"Hey, Preethy," I said, devoting too-intense attention to dialing in my locker combination. "Hey, Jamie."

Jamie stared me down with this sort of disappointed-teacher glare.

"Well, Lisa, I hope you're content with your decision to partisanize the race for student body president," she said. "I hope you've thought it through. I hope you can live with the consequences."

I shook my head in disbelief. "Is that some kind of threat?"

"I couldn't threaten you if I wanted to," she said. "I have no power. I have no social clout. I'm a Democrat in Beachside, you know. Now that you've brought political parties into the race for the first time in school history, this is how it's going to be from now on. Democrats versus Republicans. It won't be about volleyball pep rallies or antibullying campaigns or whatever the hell Nolan Ramsey has in his platform. This year, Nolan Ramsey will beat me in the election, and next year all the candidates will be Republicans, trying to out-Republican each other."

"Why are you ashamed of being a Democrat?" I said. "Why are you just throwing in the towel? Just because everybody's parents are Republicans doesn't mean *they* are."

Preethy and Jamie both looked at me with this dead-eyed "you gotta be kidding" look.

"When I ran the paper," Jamie said, "the election was a place where kids at Beachside could talk about issues that matter to us. The paper was about us. Not about who's president of the United States. And you brought that world in."

I turned away and rustled through my locker. I didn't know what to say. I was about ready to punch Jamie if she said "when I ran the paper" again. But what she was saying made sense too. Nolan had totally outsmarted me and Jamie both by going big on the GOP. Maybe I had killed the elections. Maybe she was right.

But Jamie wasn't done.

"I hope you don't have any ethical encumbrances here," she said. "Are you seeing Nolan? Because he's certainly been telling people you're interested in him."

I groaned and slammed my locker door. I almost shouted, but I knew everyone was watching, even if their faces weren't turned directly our way. "If I hear one more thing about Nolan Ramsey's sexual desires, or his imagined love life, or anything about his private thoughts, I'm going to drop out of Beachside and never come back," I said.

It was Jamie's turn to stand quiet. I could tell from the look in her eyes that she believed me. Every girl in the school would know exactly what I meant.

I headed off toward homeroom. I turned back to look at Preethy, expecting her to follow me as usual. She wasn't coming. So I headed to class alone.

Even without Preethy, there was someone in homeroom who wanted to talk to me. Breezy McFarland, whom I always thought of as "the Twirler," sat one row over in homeroom.

Breezy was on the flag line in band, and she was going to be a majorette next year when Beachside finally got majorettes. The new majorettes were largely the result of a long, intense campaign by Breezy herself, who was deeply into twirling. And the majorette corps was perfect for Breezy, who was kind of like a cheerleader but without the killer instinct. Beautiful but no snob. She talked to anybody and everybody because she was one of those people who hated silence.

"I heard about you and Nolan Ramsey," Breezy told me. "At least, I heard that you like him, and I think he likes you too. But let me tell you: he's dating this girl named Reagan. He's put her name up all over the place."

I sighed. Maybe I'd overestimated the political astuteness of the sophomore class. Maybe Jamie Scranton was right.

The entire rest of the day was uncomfortable like that. Mr. Brown, our English teacher, was having one of his near-mental-breakdown days. I don't know Mr. Brown's real story, but I like to imagine that just last year he was an eighteen-year-old Ivy League English major writing brilliant, fiery poetry. And then one morning, in some tragic *Freaky Friday* incident, he woke up as a forty-six-year-old divorced high school English teacher who could use some grooming tips. (First tip: too-long hair and a five-o-clock shadow aren't sexy on a pudgy middle-aged man.)

"Imagine for a moment that you're Hamlet's father's ghost," Mr. Brown said. "Maybe you are. A minor character that few take seriously and most don't even see. You can walk through the halls of Elsinore, you can see a family and a life that should be yours, and you can't touch any of it. And what did you do to arrive here? No, someone did something to you, took something from you. Think of that when you hear his cry for justice."

Maybe you are, he'd said. And he was right. I spent the rest of the day being basically ghosted. Preethy, my only friend really, wasn't shunning me. She sat with me at lunch, even. But she was sad and quiet, the way people are when conflict is coming and they don't like conflict. I knew that Jamie Scranton had probably already asked her to sign some kind of pact to leave me and become Jamie's friend instead. My life was becoming very Shakespearean very quickly.

In journalism class, I headed to the newspaper office to check my messages. I'd tried to get Preethy to join me—no teacher ever denies her a request for a pass out of class, because her grades are good—but apparently she had developed a sudden intense interest in chemistry lectures.

"You go on without me," she'd said. I couldn't help thinking that those were the same words a sweet, kind person like Preethy would use to break up with a long-term boyfriend.

You go on. Without me.

At least I still had my answering machine. Yes, a real answering machine, just like in the old movies, hooked up to a landline telephone in the newspaper office. Complete with a tiny cassette tape. Blanderson had demanded that I use the number for the landline as the "call the editor" number we listed in the paper.

"Students don't need to share their cell numbers with the whole world," she'd said. But deep inside I knew that little cassette tape also meant the next editor would have all the paper's messages if Blanderson fired me.

Because I am a nosy person, I was excited the first time Blanderson told me about the answering machine. I scoured the office for every tiny tape I could find, hoping to get an earful of naughty phone talk or eighties kids chatting about anti-apartheid rallies. What I found was that past editors of the paper—Jamie Scranton in particular—had led dull, phone-sexless lives. They'd gotten more thank-you calls ("Just wanted to tell you thanks for a wonderful article!") than any true journalist should. I almost erased and reused those tapes but decided I should keep them in case Jamie Scranton was ever charged with murder and needed an alibi. Yes, of course I'd clear her name. But I'd do it on the front page, in a block-buster story. We'd see who knew how to edit a paper then.

Anyway, I loved pressing the clunky little buttons like a spunky lady reporter from some 1980s cop movie or whatever.

Beeep. "Hi, this is Rhee Ann Williams. I guess I want to thank you for calling me, because, for whatever reason, the DOC hadn't contacted me yet about the execution date. Can you—can you clear up what exactly you're calling for? It sounds like you're from a newspaper, but there's not a newspaper in Beachs—"

Click. The machine didn't give you much time.

Beeep. "Hi, it's Louis East, from the *Minden Tribune-Herald.* A source in DOC—that's the Department of Corrections—is telling me that one Lisa—I don't know the last name—from the student paper there is seeking a slot at the Houser execution. I don't know if that's true, and I don't know if it's news, but I'm curious. Could you give me a call at 256-555-4193? That's Two. Five. Six. Five. Fi—"

Click.

Call me shallow, but I didn't like Louis East from the word "Hi." He had a high-pitched voice for a guy. A bit nasal. A Southern accent but not the lilting voice that so many Southern men have. I pegged him as a white guy who grew up in the suburbs of Atlanta, driving a big truck and going to a big octagonal church. An office worker with a stay-at-home wife and soft hands, the kind of guy who goes to conferences about God's plan for the family. I know I shouldn't make that sort of judgment, just from an accent. How many people have told me I must not be from here because I sound like a Yankee? But that's what I thought.

Two tough calls, and I had to make both. Where to start? What's easier, Lisa?

"Lou East, *Minden Herald*," the Atlanta-suburbs voice said. "How can I help you?"

At the start of the conversation, I almost felt like I was being processed into a doctor's office. Very basic questions. Yes, L-I-S-A. I'm in tenth grade. Blandings-Sanderson. We don't publish on a regular schedule. No, I don't have my learner's permit yet. I don't know; I'm not in a hurry to drive.

"Well, Lisa, let me say that I'm impressed with your work. I think this is an issue that bears more attention than it's getting," he said.

"I'm curious about why you're interested in it at all," I said. "Minden's like a hundred miles from here—and maybe two hundred miles from Atmore, where the execution chamber is. What's your connection to Houser?"

East sighed.

"I've been writing a lot about the drugs they use for lethal injection," he said. "The state's very secretive about it, even though state law pretty much says they have to make the information public. I put out a story a few weeks ago that speculated that their drug supply might be expired. And I guess I'm kind of worried that they set this execution date just to prove me wrong."

I couldn't help but snort out a laugh.

"They're killing a guy because of you?" I said. "At the *Minden Herald*? Isn't Minden, like, the size of Beachside? Do people outside of Benton County or whatever even read you?"

"Ever hear an actor say, 'There are no small roles, only small actors?'" East said. "Newspapers are like that. There aren't small stories or small papers. Anybody can shake things up if they work hard enough."

The conversation went on with him talking in a mildly mansplainy way about how the process would work if I did get into the execution. You went to Atmore and waited in a building inside the prison gate. You couldn't bring anything of your own past that point, even notepads and pencils. You waited for hours for word from the state supreme court and the governor. Then . . . I'll admit I wasn't listening closely. I was still marveling at this guy, this tiny-weekly-newspaper guy, talking to me like he was from the *New York Times* or something. Finally it occurred to me to ask something important.

"Are we on the record?" I said. "Are you interviewing me for a story?"

"Well, I don't know if I need to do a story," he said. "I feel like there's a story here, but I don't know. I don't have to decide today. There's lots of ethical stuff to work out here—like whether I should quote a minor and so on. It's midafternoon and I can guarantee you we won't have a story about this today. I'm always willing to talk shop, off record, with a fellow reporter. If you want, we can do that and then go on record."

He quizzed me a little longer, both off and on the record, and then we said good-bye. Talking to him had made me feel weird. On the one hand, I was a fellow reporter. On the other hand, I was a minor who couldn't be quoted. It's hard to know what to say when you don't know where you stand. Maybe this was what Jamie Scranton felt like, talking to me.

I fiddled around with *Funkirk* videos for another few minutes, trying to work up the courage to call Rhee Ann Williams. How do you start a conversation with a person about her murdered sister and grandfather? What questions do you ask? I had to think about it.

I also looked up this guy, East. Turned out he was Lew East, short for Lewis. And maybe I judged him too quickly. Small-town paper, small-town voice, but his stories were solid and full of righteous rage. AT BENTON COUNTY IMMIGRATION FACILITY, MEN DETAINED YEARS WITHOUT TRIAL. AS DEATHS BY SUICIDE SPIKE, COUNTY HAS NO PLAN TO FILL MENTAL HEALTH GAP. Letter writers and conservative blogs called him a communist, a soy boy, a *New York Times* wannabe.

And they also called him Dr. Death. In the Minden paper's archives, there were dozens of stories about East's battles to get more information about death-penalty drugs.

"The state uses three drugs to kill inmates," he wrote. "Midazolam to numb pain, rocuronium to relax the muscles, and potassium chloride to stop the heart." East had dug through court records to find the names of two drugmakers that supplied rocuronium to the state prison system. Both drug companies had later announced they would no longer sell drugs to prisons.

It was exciting. No small roles, only small actors. I felt a surge of courage. Which was good, because I had another call to make.

Ring ring.

"Hello?" said a voice. Rhee Ann sounded young but tired and weak, like she'd had a hard day. I introduced myself. Then I said: "I'll be honest. I don't want to hurt you, and I don't know how to ask questions about what you've been through. But I want to give you a chance to say your say about what's happening."

"You sound like a nice person," Rhee Ann said. "But I've been burned before by people who seem nice. And I have to admit that just before you called I was wishing that I could go back in time. That I never returned your message. Because I just saw the story in the news about how you're trying to get a seat at the execution."

"What? What story in the news?" I asked.

"I don't know," she said. "It was on TV about ten minutes ago. I think they said a newspaper reported it first. You know, I'm sure you mean well, but I've talked to a lot of media over the years, and it's never made me feel better. And I'm reluctant to talk to anybody who I think is pulling a stunt. I don't know why you'd talk to a big newspaper before you even talk to me."

I felt just sick. And then I heard my name over the school intercom. "*Please report to the vice principal's office.*"

"Trust me, this wasn't my intent," I said. "I'm . . . I'm as confused as you are about the report on TV. I didn't know anything about it. And now, just now, they're calling me to the vice principal's office. Can I call you back? If I can clear this thing up, can I give you a call back? And get an answer?"

"Sure," she said, sounding a little exasperated. "How old are you again, honey? You're in over your head. But I'm not a mean person. Call me back."

One of the great things about old-school landlines is that you can slam the phone down in loud exasperation. East! What a jerk! We'd been off the phone just minutes, and he already had a story up! Guess he'd decided he could quote a minor after all.

No time to look up the story. I'd already hit the Minden

paper's paywall anyway. I grabbed a notepad and a pen and rushed to Gordon's office.

Gordon was alone in his office scowling at an iPad. He didn't look pained this time. He looked angry.

"Wait a minute," I blurted out. "Where's Blanderson?"

Gordon stood, as if he were about to roll up his sleeves and challenge me to a fight. Then he sat back down in a huff. "Ms. Blandings-Sanderson, who I call Blandings-Sanderson because that is her name, is not here. I didn't call her to my office. I called you."

He was quiet for a moment. He didn't say, Have a seat. I sat down anyway.

"I've seen students pull a lot of stunts in my day," Gordon said. "When I was a first-year teacher, a football player streaked at graduation. There was a boy who got the mike at a school-wide assembly and claimed to be the father of a teacher's baby. And the promposals, all of them, are just way out of hand. But this is the worst stunt I've ever seen a student pull. Why would you do this to me? Why would you talk to the press about this and not even tell me?" He handed me the iPad.

I imagine the gulp in my throat was audible, like in cartoons when a mouse turns around and sees a cat. How could I explain that Lew East had stabbed me in the back?

But then I looked down at the iPad. The story on the screen wasn't from the Minden paper. It was from *Birmingham Buzz*.

SCHOOLGIRL WANTS TO SEE EXECUTION, CHALLENGES STATE.

A student newspaper editor has applied for a seat to witness the execution of Matthew John Houser, a source at the Department of Corrections told *Birmingham Buzz.*

Lisa Woodley-Rivas, the 14-year-old editor of the *Beachside Bulletin . . .*

I groaned. Schoolgirl! Fourteen? Was that supposed to be me? Someone with a crush, someone in a Catholic school uniform who giggles all the time? And why can't anybody get my name right? R-I-V-E-S, pronounced *Reeves.* Probably a French name; if it's Spanish, it's from a long time ago, maybe from some guy who washed up in Ireland from the wreck of the Spanish Armada. Still, I've been "Rivas" to people for so long that the last time Coach Jones said something stupid about immigration in class, he coughed uncomfortably and looked at me to see if I was upset.

Don't even get me started on Woodley. Yes, it's my mother's maiden name. It's also my middle name, not part of my last. I could have been Lisa Nicole or Lisa Marie, but Mom wanted to provide two-step authentication to anyone who might claim I was Not Really From Around Here. Woodley is my microchip, proof I'm a Southerner.

"Dr. Gordon, I didn't seek out this story," I said. "If you read it really closely, you'll see that their source is someone at Corrections. I bet I know who. And you'll notice they didn't talk to me to confirm it. Did they call you? Look at this! I don't even see any mention of their having tried to call me or you. I think the journalism you have a problem with is theirs, not mine."

"It's not their journalism that's going to get me a bunch of calls from angry parents," Gordon said.

"Well, actually, it is, but I see what—"

"*Just be quiet!*" Gordon said. "Look, I don't want to have

to give you or Ms. Blandings-Sanderson some kind of order. I don't want to defund or cancel the paper. I don't want to have to invoke my right, under the Supreme Court decision in *Hazelwood v. Kuhlmeier*, to review and edit the school newspaper. I want to have a collegial relationship, where we all talk to each other and reason together as professionals."

"You just shouted at me to be quiet," I noted.

"Well, let's start again," he said. "Lisa, just talk to me a little about why you're so fascinated with seeing someone die. Is everything all right at home? Is there some sort of abuse or neglect?"

I'm sure I rolled my eyes. Since when had anybody around here cared about my crappy homelife? Teachers never ask you about your feelings until you steal, stab, and rob.

"My home is Alabama," I said. "Why is Alabama so fascinated with killing people? Why do they invite journalists to come see it? And if they're inviting people to come see it, why can't I? No, things aren't all right. My home is weird."

Gordon seemed to deflate a little, his face looking a little less red.

"Is this just a way to get attention?" he asked. "Is that what it is? Are you trying to impress Nolan Ramsey? I hear that you're kind of sweet on him."

My brain exploded. I'm sure Gordon didn't see it. It was like dynamite going off in a safe. My head probably jolted a little to one side, maybe with some smoke coming out of my ears. But most of the force was contained inside my skull.

"Nolan Ramsey," I said through gritted teeth. "Do you have any idea what kind of hell it is to be a girl at this school you run? People coming on to you, sexually harassing you, and then telling vicious lies about you? And then when I'm trying to just do my job, the vice principal joins in on all the sexual harassing?"

I pulled out my phone and held it out like Princess Leia holding her thermal detonator. "If I hear Nolan Ramsey's name from you one more time, I'll Me Too you so fast you won't know whether to shit or go blond. Good day."

As I got up, Gordon looked dumbfounded. It wasn't just shock. There was also a look of confusion, as if I'd said everything in Spanish and he was still trying to translate.

"Blind," Blanderson said later. "The phrase is 'Shit or go blind.'"

"Oh, God," I said, blushing. "I don't know how many times I've said this to people. I thought . . . I should have known. When Mom cusses, she always has a more country accent. . . . But wait a minute. How does that make sense? Going blind isn't a choice. Pooping and bleaching your hair—those are both things you do in a bathroom."

"I think you're reading too much into it," Blanderson said.

"So what's your take on the Me Too threat?" I asked. "Was that a dirty thing to do? Did I misuse Me Too? Am I a bad sister?"

"I'm not going to criticize another woman's choices on that," Blanderson said. "I will say this, though. As journalists, we have an extra responsibility to be thoughtful when we use media. It's almost never a good idea to release an accusation or make a claim because you're angry, and it's never right to do it to settle a score. And, to be fair, have you ever tried to bring your problems with Nolan to Gordon's attention before this? So when I put my journalist hat on, no, it's not ideal."

I planted my face in my hands.

"I thought you were going to say that," I said. "What you're saying is I did the wrong thing. What now? What do I do to fix it?"

"My advice? Nothing. Just let it sit. He's not going to run around and tell someone what you said. You shouldn't breathe a word of it either. Just go on like it never happened. Maybe you've scared him off."

"And what if he's right?" I said. "What if there are people out there who are going to attack him, and you, for me doing this?"

"In journalism, the answer is always tomorrow's paper," Blanderson said. "We'll work our way out of it. We need to release a new edition of the paper soon, and that edition needs to show that you're approaching this as a true citizen. Show them you can understand the human story here. By the way, how's that interview with Rhee Ann Williams coming?"

Door

Rhee Ann opened the door before I even got there. I guess she was one of those people who watched when they knew they had company coming. An introvert.

"Come on in, sweetie," she said, stepping back into the darkness and waving a beckoning hand. It was as if I wasn't even there to see her but instead was a friend of her daughter, just passing through the den on my way to gossip in the bedroom.

Rhee Ann didn't look the way I expected. She was Mom's age, with short straight hair that was dyed and highlighted. Tasteful silver jewelry. Brown slacks and a ruffly white shirt. A slightly formal, feminine, intelligent look. Like Mom when she's showing a house or one of those education professors who observes your Spanish teacher from the back of the class. I suppose I'd expected "typing-class girl," still with big hair and a print dress like the girls in the old yearbook. And I have to say, there was something about her current look that didn't seem right on her. Her clothes said responsibility and accomplishment and slow cooking of good food. But her eyes looked troubled and preoccupied and weary. Like the women who smoke cigarettes in the Walmart parking lot waiting for a Megabus.

"Sorry, I was just putting the beagle away," she said. "He's a rascal."

And just as my eyes were adjusting to the dark, she did the most unusual, disarming thing. She took my hand in her soft hand. Then the other. She sort of glowed, looking at me as if I were her own child.

"Beautiful," she said. "You look like her. I can see it."

I almost asked if she meant I looked like her sister. I'm so glad I said nothing.

"Your mom was always one of the prettiest girls in school," she continued. "Almost too pretty, if it's possible to be too pretty. I think it is." She brushed the hair away from my eyes. "It's better to dial it back just a smidge. You're stunning, but someone has to look at you for a few seconds to get the full effect."

I chuckled, and maybe my eyes watered a little. Nobody tells me I'm pretty.

"Can I get you a Coke or a tea?" She dashed off to the kitchen before I could even answer, motioned me into her living room. "Is that your real hair color, or do you dye it black? But then, your dad's from Mexico or somewhere, right? Is Lisa your name or a nickname? Is there something Spanish that it's short for?"

"Just Lisa," I said. "I don't really need anything."

"Water then, just in case," she called from the kitchen.

Her living room seemed impossibly nice, considering there was a dog living here. On the hearth, little vases with fabric dandelions and daisies next to scented candles that had never been lit. A doggy bed sat near the hearth with a single unchewed toy in it, like a memorial to a dead dog rather than the bed of a beagle who was just in the garage or something. There was an actual coffee-table book on the coffee table, with panoramic photos of the coast of Italy. All the furniture looked proper and delicate and uncomfortable, except for one recliner against the wall, too close to the wall to open and recline. In a little basket next to the recliner, a paperback mystery with a bright cover and a pair of drugstore reading glasses. It didn't take me long to realize that Rhee Ann had prepared for me like I was company: normally the chair would have been out closer to the TV, footrest extended while Rhee Ann read and the Braves game droned on in the background.

I was looking at the pictures on the mantel when Rhee Ann came into the room with a water for me and a tea for herself.

"It's just me and Darwin," she said, motioning to the beagle's bed. "That one with the moustache, he's my ex-husband. Long gone. Where? I don't really care. That one's my daughter. Off to college, but she comes home to wash clothes every weekend. Obsessed with softball and baseball, don't hardly say boo to anybody. And here's Jennifer. It sounds weird, but at my age I don't miss her as much as I miss the kids I assume she would have had. It would have been nice to have had some cousins around for Britt. A whole bunch of girls having a sleepover here. I imagine them all coming over for a visit, just on a whim, when Britt's off at college. Why don't we do this at the table? Britt always did her homework at the table. And you're going to have to take notes."

Rhee Ann seemed to sense that I was nervous. She started talking again before we were even completely seated.

"So," she said. "What is it you want to know? And please, let me give you some advice: don't ever ask people how they feel. That's the worst question a reporter can ask. I mean, how do you feel right now? Hard, isn't it?"

I scratched the first question off my list.

"So, tell me about Jennifer," I said. "What was she like?"

Rhee Ann crossed her arms and looked away with a sigh.

"That's the other one they always ask," she said. "I have to tell you, it's hard. Even with someone you love, it's hard, after a while, to remember. To remember everything. To remember what's important and what's not important. Almost every day I hear something that was an in-joke between me and her—when somebody says, 'Nip it in the bud,' I always want to turn to her and giggle—but there's nobody there to get the joke.

"When I think now about who she was, I think that she wasn't really Jennifer Williams. She didn't have a chance to be. I mean, she and I used to play cootie catcher—you know the little four-sided paper-puppet thing where you pick a number and a letter and lift up a flap and there's your fortune? We used to play that, and she could never really decide what she wanted. Did she want to live in Paris or New York or here? Did she want to marry a preacher or a doctor? Those things never work, because you don't write all the possible futures under the flaps. There are lots of futures you never think of. Happy alone? That's a future. Work for the state for twenty-five years, retire at forty-seven? That's a future.

"I think she was aware of that. I think there were paths in life that she wanted to take, and she knew they were there, but nobody had really put them in front of her. You know, she was the only girl I ever knew who didn't ever make her Barbies, you know, do it. But when that came up on nature shows, with animals doing it, she never made jokes or turned away or anything like other people did. Even when animals got eaten. When a baby animal got caught by a predator. She didn't flinch. She was just fascinated. She loved science and

I think she might have wanted to go into biology. But, you know, there's the whole evolution thing. There would have had to have been a fight there. I could imagine her wanting to go to college to study biology and my parents telling her it wasn't God's plan for her life. I could imagine that happening. But it didn't happen. It didn't happen, because she went to her grandpa's house to check in on him, and a man walked out the front door and shot her in the head. No particular reason. She didn't do anything wrong or unwise or anything a safety expert would tell you not to do. But she suddenly ceased to be. The rest of my sister's life didn't happen."

"I get . . . I get the feeling you don't like to talk about this," I said. "I mean any of this. Even the good stuff about her life and who she was."

"As I get older, I like talking less," she said. "About everything. There's a sorrow that goes beyond where words can go. Talking, describing it again, doesn't help. Everything that can be said, about the good and the bad, love and hate, it's all been said. Life is like a little boat that's been out on the ocean a long time. I've been seasick for a long time, but I've learned how to live with it. Sometimes it's better to deal with the seasickness in silence."

There was an awkward moment as I struggled to finish writing that down.

"So if you don't like talking," I asked, "why did you agree to talk to me?"

"Because I have to," she said. "Don't you see? I'm the victim's family. I have to do this every time he comes up for execution. Every time, I have to make the case that her murderer deserves to be killed."

"And if you don't? I mean, aren't there prosecutors and all

that to make this go through even if you don't want to weigh in?"

Rhee Ann shook her head vigorously.

"I mean, there *are*," she said. "But . . . Look. I'm a nice person. I believe in God. Now, I don't believe in everything everybody tells me about God. I don't know how many people have told me, since Jennifer was killed, how many people have told me that God shut a door in my life and will open another. God didn't shut that door. God didn't shut my sister."

She noticed her fist was clenched, and then she laid both hands flat on the table in front of her.

"So, I believe in God. I understand the people who say God made everybody and doesn't want anybody to be killed. Believe me, I do. But those people—if they're the only ones talking, then the whole conversation is going to be about Houser, about how awful his childhood was, about how he's completely crazy and pitifully stupid and no logical person would have done what he did. And it's true. It's all true. He threw his life away, as well as my grandfather's and my sister's, and it was tragically dumb. But if they're the only ones who talk, then the story is about him, and my sister gets crowded out of the conversation. I'm just not going to let that happen. Even if I can't think of what to say, I'll hold this space for her.

"But I'm a nice person. That's what makes me so upset sometimes. I'm a nice person with a dog, a person who likes to read. I don't deserve this either. I don't deserve to be the woman in the newspaper who's asking to have a man killed. I didn't ask to be in this position. It's the position he put me in."

Again, a pause while I took notes. Sometimes looking down at the page is the only thing that keeps me from freaking out.

"I almost hate to ask this," I said. "Maybe it's not right,

but . . . if Alabama didn't have the death penalty, if he got life without parole instead of the death penalty . . . I mean, it seems to me that you wouldn't be in this position in that case. If he got life instead of death, wouldn't he just be forgotten, rotting away in prison?"

Rhee Ann threw her hands up.

"Sure," she said. "I mean, yeah. But that isn't what happened."

"Do you ever wish that it *was* what happen—"

"That door is shut too," she said. "It is what it is. I was still a child when the verdict came down. I didn't know what it meant. I'm sure I would have asked for death, and a worse death than this, if anybody asked me, but nobody asked me. That door is shut, and it won't ever come open."

"Again, I'm sorry, but—" I began, and then started over. "Look, I like you a lot. I don't want to hurt you, and I don't really have an opinion on the death penalty. But I do think what you're saying actually sounds like an argument against the death penalty. I mean, there are other states in which that door doesn't shut."

She shook her head slowly and looked at me with genuine affection.

"Sweetie," she said. "I like you too. So pretty. So smart. But one day—I hate to say it—it will happen to you too. Not like this, I hope, but one day somebody will shut a door in your face that will never open again. And you'll understand. You'll see what I'm saying. You'll see what it's like for your life to become less and never become more again."

Ketchup

I watched Blanderson's face as she read the story. And Preethy's too. We were still a team, the three of us, meeting in Blanderson's room after school. Still a team, no matter how often Dr. Gordon and Jamie Scranton seemed to be looking over our shoulders.

"This is excellent," Blanderson said. "This is very, very good work. Her quotes are powerful."

I knew it was good. If Blanderson had looked at it and just grunted, I still would have known. It was a powerful feeling, like getting into one of those big pickup trucks where you have to step on the side rail to get up into the cab. I felt like I was looking over all the other traffic.

"I think it would be more powerful with a shorter lead," Blanderson said. "Every writer wants to set the scene with a description. Sometimes it says more about the writer than it does about the subject. So what if she has photos in her house? What if you just jump right in? What's the key point of the story?"

Blanderson's criticism didn't even hurt.

"I'm trying to show that Rhee Ann is a nice person," I said. "She doesn't want to be in the position of asking for this man to be killed, but she feels like she has to."

"Open with that," Blanderson said.

"Sounds a little too direct," I said.

"Try it and see," Blanderson said. "What do you think, Preethy? How do you like it?"

Preethy looked at me with a pained expression, as if she desperately wanted to say something tender and intimate but couldn't break through some barrier. Then she turned to Blanderson. Safer, I guess.

"I think you're right," she said. "I think the narrator is too much in the picture. I can't explain it exactly. I think we're drawing too much attention to ourselves as reporters. I think we need a more, I don't know, newspapery tone. Sorry, Lisa. As a reader I want to feel like I'm looking through you, not at you."

"Of course," I said. "Why stop now?"

In the last few days, I hadn't become entirely invisible to Preethy, but I was slowly becoming see-through, like the imperiled hero in some time-travel comedy. The only difference was I didn't know where to go back in time, what point in history to change, to make myself solid again.

Blanderson leaned back in her chair, pulling away from the paper to get a good look at the two of us. "Okayyyy. . . ." she said, just realizing something was different.

"I tell you what will make this story pop," Blanderson said. "What will take it from good to great. A profile of a victim's family member is a great thing. It can stand alone, if we take care to provide some balance. But what's even better is a side-by-side piece. A victim's family member here and an advocate for Houser here. His lawyer, or a death-penalty opponent. Both sides of the debate, personified. We can weave them together in one story or run them as companion pieces. Lisa, what role have you envisioned for Preethy in all of this? Because I could see Preethy writing that half of the story. Teamwork."

I flushed a little. I hadn't envisioned any sort of role for Preethy in this work. It was all my project. No wonder she was drifting away.

"I'm not sure I . . ." Preethy started. "I thought my role would be to write the normal newspaper stuff. To fill the paper with news that's actually about the school, like normal. Frankly, I'm not entirely comfortable with any of this. And you know what? Neither of you really asked me before going ahead with any of this."

I knew she was right. Why don't I think before I open my big mouth? Why do I instantly go on the attack, like Mom?

"We talked about this," I said. "We talk about everything. Or we used to. Hours on the phone, hours at your house. I know I told you what I was planning to do."

"Nobody *asked* me," Preethy said. "If you'd *asked* me, I would have said that the obvious reason to print a special edition would be to do more coverage of the student body president election. There's a debate coming up. That's what I'd like to cover. The debate."

I chuckled. Preethy looked hurt.

"I mean, come on, Preethy," I said. "As close as you are to Jamie now, should you be covering that?"

"Let me—let me stop you right there," Blanderson said. "I don't know what's going on here, but I do know that in a school with ninety people in its graduating class, there's little room for finger-pointing about conflicts of interest. And, Lisa, consider this: you're going to need art for page one. You can get a photo of the debate. Did you get a photo of Rhee Ann at the interview? Do you want to go back and ask for one?"

I just shook my head. Blanderson sighed.

"This is the toughest part of journalism," she said. "It's about coaxing people to talk, which is ultimately about relationships. And relationships, as you can see, are hard."

There's nothing like a little real-life drama to make American History homework seem engrossing. At home, I headed straight up to my bedroom and zipped through a chapter about Texas and California being admitted to the union. But when I opened my laptop to start my assignment, there was an email from Lew East. "Thought you might need this," the subject line said.

It was former governor Fischer King's own file on the Houser execution. Lew explained that when a death sentence is sent to the governor for final approval, lawyers for the state include a file for the governor to look over to make sure he or she wants to go ahead with the move. Years ago, King got Houser's file and cleared him to die. A federal court stopped the execution and let Houser have another appeal. When Governor King left office a couple of years ago, all his papers were moved to the state's Department of Archives and History, where Lew went and dug up the files on Houser and the other six people King had cleared for execution.

"There's a psychological profile in there that's marked CON-FIDENTIAL," Lew wrote. "Don't worry about that. Once it's in the archives, it's public record."

Of course, the confidential file was the first attachment I opened. The first pages were very old, typewritten stuff from the nineties. The psychologist who interviewed Houser just after his arrest made note of the Dungeons & Dragons defense—the claim by Houser's lawyers that role-playing games made him do it—but in an interview with the shrink, Houser hardly mentioned the game. Mostly he talked about his supposed business making dice and wooden figurines of *Lord of the Rings* characters for nerds with too much money.

"HOUSER appeared comfortable with the interviewer and sometimes overly confident," the report read. "He boasted about his sports car and claimed to make $80,000 per year selling handmade items to role-playing gamers. He claimed to have had sexual relations with roughly two dozen women in Beachside, saying they were very attracted to his intellect. He demanded to know his intelligence score and seemed very disappointed to learn it was lower than he had anticipated."

I flipped through to find his test results. Houser's IQ was 84, which put him in the bottom 14 percent of human beings.

There was also a psychiatric interview, done some years later. Houser still bragged about his intelligence after years in prison, but now he seemed "socially awkward, shy, and anxious. He expressed concern about not being tough enough to survive in the general prison population were his death sentence to be overturned. He also expressed fear that, on execution, he would die without ever having had sexual relations with a woman."

Sick and sad, that's how I felt. It seemed as though Houser had thrown away his life, and the lives of Jennifer Williams and her grandfather, not because he was crazy or abused or desperate but just because he was stupid. Stupid and egotistical and maybe desperate because it's hard to maintain your egotism when you're stupid. He told the psychiatrist he'd wanted to steal a bunch of gold, a large pile of real gold, because it was a great prize, a great feat, like something from a movie. And he'd chosen old man Williams as his victim simply because he'd heard a rumor, an offhand mention, that the man was stockpiling guns and gold. He'd gone into the house, demanded that Williams show him the gold, then shot him when Williams said there wasn't any. Then he'd shot Jennifer on his way out. Surely the difference between life and death couldn't be as flimsy as this. One decision by one dumb person.

My email binged again. "Lisa, this is Violet Takeda. I'm part of Matthew Houser's defense team. I know it's after hours, but I can talk now if you want to give me a call." At the bottom of the email, a number with an area code that, once I looked it up, seemed to be from New York City. I also found a bio of Violet on the website of a New York law firm. A recent graduate of Yale Law, young and pretty with triple piercings on just one ear that looked out of place with her dark business suit. Part of the firm's "well-known pro bono team." I'd read enough by that time to know that death-row inmates often had lawyers from big firms, which have whole offices dedicated to representing impoverished inmates for free. And I'd read enough to know that this, to law students, was a very cool job. Violet Takeda probably Jamie Scrantoned for years to get to this case.

"This is going to sound cheesy," Takeda told me over the phone later, "but when I was young, I saw the film version of *To Kill a Mockingbird,* and I thought this was the kind of law I wanted to do. I guess it's kind of ironic that this case, which is really the first case I've been on here, is from Alabama. But I need to note that I'm new to Houser. I'm the low person on the ladder in a very big team. Frankly, that's why I'm the one who's taking your call."

I chuckled. "It sounds like you're telling me I'm not that important," I said.

She laughed.

"Maybe I'm telling you we're both in the same boat," she said. "You're important to me. I'm important to me. People at the top don't always know what's really important. By the way, I read about what you're doing in terms of trying to get in to view the execution. Impressive."

"The worldwide reach of *Birmingham Buzz*," I said.

"No," she said. "No, I don't think so. I want to say you were mentioned in the *New York Times'* last story on the execution. This morning. You should look it up."

Jeez, I thought. Gordon is going to poop a brick *and* go blind.

"Well, look, I'm going to dive right in," I said. "You're in this business because of *To Kill a Mockingbird*. You want to defend the innocent. But nobody here is arguing that Houser is innocent. I mean, he killed these two people. Nobody's even arguing that he had a good reason, like self-defense. Don't you think this is a little far from being Atticus Finch?"

"No, I don't," Takeda said. "Because what does Atticus say in court? That the law makes everyone equal. That everyone deserves a fair trial. And this case, like so many cases, shows just how unequal and bizarre and biased the death penalty is. I mean, the guy has a subnormal IQ. There's strong evidence that he's schizophrenic, but the state psychologist never conducted an assessment for that. Houser barely knows what planet he's on."

"I'm not sure I see the bias here," I said. "I mean, he's a white guy who shot two people, one to get a bunch of money and the other to cover up his crime. He's never argued that he didn't do it. He's never argued that he didn't do it for money, which is pretty cold."

"Well, here's the mother of all bias in the court system: the ability to pay a good lawyer," Takeda said. "And that's what Houser very much didn't have. His lawyer back then went ahead with this Dungeons & Dragons defense, which was complete BS, a total gimmick unfounded in the facts. I think the idea was that Mr. Houser would blame the game on the stand, then beg for mercy and claim that he'd had a born-again experience or something. But Houser wasn't willing to do that, because D&D wasn't ever a big part of his life. It actually turned the jury members against Mr. Houser. It branded him as someone who might be a Satanist. And the state psychologist, amazingly, went in there trying to find out if D&D actually caused Mr. Houser's insanity—when the psychological community didn't recognize, then or now, any kind of role-playing-related illnesses. He's never, to this day, had a legitimate psychological examination."

A little pause while I typed all this up.

"Sorry, I'm just writing all this down," I said. "You know, I sat down a few days ago with Rhee Ann Williams, whose sister and grandfather were killed by Mr. Houser. She still seems devastated by the whole thing. And she wants Houser to die so she can stop responding to court motions and execution dates. How does that . . ." Somehow it seemed right to say it this time. "How does that make you feel?"

Takeda was quiet for a moment.

"You know, I'm saddened, but not surprised, to hear that she's still very hurt by this," Takeda said. "What she's gone through must be horrifying, and it's a horror only some people can fully understand. I really do not want to be in conflict with Rhee Ann Williams. I don't want to cause her any harm. But if we're going to do this very serious thing, as a society, if we're going to take a life, we have to make sure we give everybody real and effective representation. We have to answer all the questions."

"I have to say, when this runs alongside the comments from Rhee Ann, I think your objections to the execution are going to sound very technical and legalistic," I said.

"Well, we're talking about law here," she said. "We're talking about using the law to kill someone. People love to talk about the thousands of pages of arguments we've filed to prevent this execution. Remember that for every page we've filed to prevent this from happening, the state has filed a page of equally complex legalistic arguments saying he should be killed. I can tell you that when you're in an execution chamber, watching someone slowly be poisoned, it's not the defense that looks legalistic. It's the prosecution."

There was so much going on that day that I forgot it was Thursday, the day Dad comes home for the weekend. Since I was a little girl, I've waited for him on Thursday nights, watching TV on the couch by the window. Even now that my parents are "middle-aged" and crazy and every conversation is like talking through a rusty drive-in speaker, I tend to wait up for him, as if Young Dad will arrive, and Baby Lisa too, and we'll build Lego cities on the coffee table the way we used to.

Not this time. I was at the kitchen table, trying desperately to catch up on my backlog of homework, when Dad stepped through the front door with his bags, ungreeted by anyone. There was a folded newspaper under his arm and a big smile on his face.

"My famous daughter!" he said. "In the *New York Times*! How cool is that?"

"I don't understand you," Mom said to him, putting down

her iPad and hiding her glasses in her pocket. "Why don't you ever knock? Lisa could have opened the door for you."

This thing, to knock or not to knock, was one of their many ongoing fights, fights that went back to deep disagreements about how life should be lived. Dad never knocks, not at home. He unlocks the door no matter how much he's carrying. And he locks the door behind him even when he's just taking the garbage out to the curb. Mom always knocks if someone's home, and she'll wait for a full minute or more for Dad or me to open the door, even if she has a key in hand. "It's the principle of the thing," she says. She's never told me what the principle is, but I know. A husband should always open the door for his Beloved Wife to show that she's still his cherished lover, the one he wants to protect. And a child should always do as a Southern Mother asks, because *Ma'am*. Had I been born a boy, she would have taught me the lessons Dad never learned, lessons about how Southern boys are supposed to love and revere their mothers with Elvis-like chivalry. Somehow I'm a failure both as a girl and as a boy.

Dad has his own unreasonable demands in this ongoing lifestyle war. He thinks everything should be streamlined in this house he barely lives in. He thinks the beds should be harder. None of his tastes are actually matters of taste, or so he claims. They have roots in Army training or engineering or "I could tell you, but I'd have to kill you." When you call from the grocery store to ask if we need ketchup, he'll say no, even though we're out, because Ketchup Is Not a Need. The same with dryer sheets, because static cling is a fleeting state, not a significant problem. Which he says with all the ignorance of someone who's never worn women's clothing. At least, he hasn't as far as I know, but maybe I don't know him any better than I know the dads on TV. There for an episode, offscreen most of the time. His greatest accomplishment as a husband is not getting canceled.

"So I'm at work, and my co-worker comes to me and says, 'Wow, is this your daughter in the *New York Times?*'" Dad said. "And look. It is. My daughter the famous journalist."

He handed the folded paper to Mom. By this point, I'd already read the article online, a four-paragraph story about Houser's latest court appeal. The very last paragraph read: "The department is also considering a request by Lisa W. Rives, editor of the student newspaper at Beachside High School, for a seat at the execution. The state typically sets aside a seat for the local newspaper in the victim's hometown, but Beachside's last newspaper ceased publication more than a decade ago."

Mom covered her face when she read it.

"Oh, God," she said. "This is horrifying. At least it's W. Rives. I'll let your name be on it. I don't want anybody to know a Woodley is doing this."

Dad shrugged.

"Sweetie, this is an accomplishment," he said to her. "Lisa's doing journalism that catches the attention of the nation's best newspaper. She's writing about important things, and she's only fifteen. It's like a high school baseball player playing in the major leagues."

Mom snorted. "Just what everyone wants, a daughter who pitches for the Braves."

"Well, if she pitched for the Braves, wouldn't you be proud?"

"Yes," Mom said. "Yes, I would. Because her name and her family's name would be up there next to Hank Aaron and Dale Murphy and all sorts of people everybody knows and respects. Instead, her name's in the paper with Matthew Houser, of all people. I don't see why neither of you cares about your reputation here, your reputation with people you can see and touch. You don't understand the very basics of how people interact with each other. There's something wrong with both of you."

Dad rolled his eyes like a ten-year-old.

"Not the autism-spectrum thing again," he said. "I've been tested. She's been tested."

"I've been tested for autism?" I asked, but nobody was listening to me. It was like I wasn't in the room.

"Autistic, Yankee, I can't tell the difference," Mom said. "Neither of you seems to be able to read other people's emotions. Simple cues! Neither of you understands that in a small town, you have to polish your reputation like a mirror. It's a survival skill. Juliette Hampton Morgan!"

I threw my hands up in exasperation.

"Mom, Juliette Hampton Morgan was a *hero*," I said. "She's like one of five white people I can think of in Alabama who was actually against segregation back then."

"She committed suicide," Mom said. "She didn't get married. She didn't have children to pass along her legacy. She just wrote all these letters to the *Montgomery Advertiser* without thinking about how it would affect her family. Don't you think her parents said she should stop and think about a better way to do this? And she didn't listen. And she ruined her reputation and became the Crazy Library Lady."

"I'm sorry," Dad said. "Who is Juliette Hampton Morgan?"

"It's from Alabama History class, Dad," I said. "Don't worry about it."

"Honey," Mom said, taking my face in her hands. "Honey, I'm just trying to understand why you don't want to be a girl. A fifteen-year-old. You'll have, like, fifty years to do grown-up stuff. Really hard adult things. Why jump in now? Now is a time to chase boys, buy lovely clothes, and enjoy your body. Dream about ten thousand futures."

"Mom, that's what *you* want," I said. "I don't want to be fifteen. It's not fun for me. Because I'm not, you know, Selena Gomez or whoever's in the old Disney-movie version of high school you have in your head. I've seen your yearbook. I understand how cool you were. It's not like that for me."

I think I touched a nerve with Mom. Her eyes softened, and I was worried that she was about to hug me and promise to give me a Disney-movie makeover. Luckily, Dad interrupted the moment.

"Who's Selena Gomez?" he said.

We both just looked at him like he was an idiot.

Mom turned away, looked out the window.

"Where is this thing going to be done, anyway?" she said after a minute.

"Holman Prison," I said. "In Atmore."

Suddenly Mom brightened.

"Atmore," she said. "Like where the Creek casino is?"

"Umm . . . yeeeah," I said.

"Well, that's like five hours from here," she said. "So there's no way you can go. Can't drive yourself, and I won't drive you. And I won't let *him* drive you."

I looked at Dad, but he was suddenly lost in the glow of his phone.

"Whoa, Selena Gomez," he said, holding up his phone so we could see a photo. "She's *fifteen*?"

"She hasn't been fifteen in a long time," Mom said. "Not that that matters to *men*. Lovers of the young flesh."

"Jeez," Dad said. "That came out of nowhere."

He looked to me for comfort and found none.

"Did it, Dad?" I said. "Did it really?"

"Perhaps I should clarify," Dad said, scanning us both. "Never mind. Look, I don't see why I can't take some time off work, if it's during the week, to drive you."

"What date is the thing?" Mom asked. Dad pointed to the paper, which she was still holding. "Ah, there. Look. You'll be at Nellis. In Las Vegas. At that conference. With Denise. So no luck there."

"Crap," Dad said. "We're supposed to do a presentation."

"Maybe you could back out and let Denise do the presentation alone," I suggested.

"No," Mom said, matter-of-factly. "There's no point in Denise going if your dad doesn't go."

"What's that supposed to mean?" I said. Though I was pretty sure I knew what that meant.

Just then, a jangle—a heart-stoppingly loud jangle—on the landline phone. The Denise phone.

"I'll get it," Dad said.

"Go ahead. Run away," Mom said. "If you withdraw, I win."

Mom and I stood there uncomfortably while Dad got the phone. In my mind, so many questions. I didn't know what to say.

"Lisa," Dad said. "It's for you."

Even more questions. The only call I wanted in all the world was a teary invitation from Preethy to come over and play. She was the only good thing about being fifteen, the only person who could make me want to be even younger. But she never called our landline.

"Lisa Rivas?" a voice asked. "I'm calling from the Educational Press Law Center. We think you have a strong case for a seat at this execution. We were wondering if you'd like to take that case to court."

Face

It occurs to me now that before I became a journalist, my life was boring. In a good way. I didn't really do anything; I didn't really *make* anything. Long lazy afternoons on Preethy's bed with its puffy duvet, reading manga and telling jokes. Preethy working on her long-term plan—maybe a twenty-year plan—to become someone who draws eyes for a living. Me still shopping around for a plan. The two of us watching countless movies as I tried to decide who I want to be when I grow up. Hard-nosed prosecutor? Wiccan priestess who marries a rock star? Earnest aid worker bringing medicine to peasants in the mountains? Mama anthropologist, leading a squadron of college students through a Dig of Monumental Importance at a secret site hidden from potential looters? It had seemed, just a year or two earlier, like I had a lot of runway before I had to pick a grown-up life. Then I could even still sink back into daydreams of my ideal life path: discovering a giant, docile, magical animal in the woods behind my house, clinging to its fur as we flew above the mountains. Watching those movies with Preethy, I might as well have been playing with dolls like a little kid.

After I became editor of the newspaper, though, things started happening so fast I could barely plan the rest of my week, much less the next week or ten years from then. That Friday, the day after my call from the Educational Press Law Center, was the day the craziness truly kicked in.

First: Mom misplaced her glasses, which meant that even though I was ready and at the door with my backpack by 6:50, we had to spend ten minutes tearing the house up looking for them. Finally, Mom had to roust Dad out of bed to drive me. Dad came out of the bedroom looking, in my opinion, rather skeevy in his workout clothes. Bicycle shorts and a T-shirt and Crocs.

"Um, do I look okay to go out?" he mumbled.

"You look like a CEO who's getting arrested," I said. "Why can't old men in America wear smoking jackets or samurai kimono or something?"

"I won't get out of the car," Dad said.

So we got to school right at 7:20, just before bell and anthem time, and there were a bunch of kids holding a protest in the parking lot—big banners that read BAND FOR RAMSEY and NO NEW PEP RALLIES and maybe six or eight kids standing around or leaning on trombone cases.

"Dad," I said, "let me out over there. I want to see what's going on."

They were all kids I knew from the band bus, low brass and percussion and that one saxophone the band director was always chewing out. Exactly the band kids who'd actually have the guts to be late for class to be in a protest. When I asked what it was about, they directed me to Mackayla Cotney, the only girl in the group. She's the pit percussion section leader and the household deity of an otherwise all-male tribe of lanky, nerdy Napoleons.

"We're protesting Jamie Scranton's plan to hold more pep rallies," she told me. I didn't have my reporter's notebook, so I had to scribble what she said down in my math notebook.

"I think it's great that Jamie wants more attention for the volleyball team," Mackayla continued. "But they're not the only unsung heroes at the school. We band nerds have lives, and we work hard, and we think Jamie should have asked us before proposing *more* pep rallies for *more* teams where we do the all work and get none of the attention."

"Besides," said one of the trombones, his Adam's apple bobbing, "it's just volleyball."

"Be quiet, man," Mackayla said. "Let me do the talking here."

The bell rang. I could see Dr. Gordon and the school resource officer making their way down the hill to discipline us all. Gordon was walking with his chest puffed out, like a man determined to lay down the law.

Then the anthem started. You could hear it faintly in the background. Mackayla turned toward the school's flagpole and snapped a crisp Girl Scout salute. Reflexively, I came to attention too, holding my notebook up against my chest with a flat hand. And Gordon and the resource officer, realizing what was going on, turned and put their hands on their hearts too.

"Now's your chance, dummies," Mackayla said to her lackeys. "Put down the banners, and make your getaway. If you can sneak past Gordon, maybe you won't get suspended."

The trombones and tubas were quiet for a second.

"But it's the anthem," one of them said.

"Don't be an idiot," Mackayla said.

"But we're Republicans," another said.

Mackayla turned, still saluting, and glared at him. Then I heard the sound of banner poles being thrown into the back of a truck, the rattle of trombone cases being picked up, the pitter-patter of giant clumsy feet running away.

Just Mackayla and I remained, at attention. Our nation's anthem is uncomfortably long.

"So," Mackayla said, at about the time of the rocket's red glare, "is that your mom's new boyfriend who dropped you off? 'Cause he's a looker."

Gross.

"That's my *dad*," I said. I could have said more. I don't believe in slut shaming or the language that surrounds it. But there are some very improper names I'd like to call these *people* who keep creeping on my old man.

"Like stepdad? When did your mom get remarried?" Mackayla said.

"Same dad I've always had," I said.

We heard the gravel crunch of a car pulling up behind us. I hoped it wasn't cops, preparing to take us away.

Mackayla shrugged. "Okay, real dad. Don't see him around much."

"He's been around," I said. "Been around the whole time."

"Funny," she said. "I think I'd remember him. That gray-sideburns thing is a good look. Like a TV news anchorman or whatever."

The anthem ended. Turning, I saw a local TV van, with one of those satellite antenna things, behind us. A news guy in a suit and a camera guy in shorts were standing there, still at attention.

"I'm out," I said. "This is too much crazy for seven thirty. You're in luck, Mackayla. Your own TV news guy."

Gordon was on us almost immediately, but he rushed past and went straight to the news guys.

"Can I help you gentlemen?" he nearly shouted. "There was a small event here, but it's over and we're not taking interviews."

News guy: "Actually, we were here to ask for an interview with Lisa Rivas Woodley."

"Peace," I said to the resource officer, shouldering my backpack and heading up the hill to school.

"You gentlemen need to leave the premises," Gordon said. "You don't have permission to be here. And you students need to come to my office. Including the one who's leaving."

I continued up the hill as if I hadn't even heard him. Was he really going to chase me down in front of the TV guys?

"*You'll still have a tardy!*" Gordon shouted.

I did. And the day got worse from there. In history class I got a zero on a big paper about Claudette Colvin and Rosa Parks, a topic I truly cared about, because I had forgotten about the assignment. For two or three weeks.

In math, I realized the back of my homework was covered with notes from the parking lot protest.

And of course, eating lunch by yourself is also fun. As I stared down at the Styrofoam, I had a sudden urge to go sit at the teachers' table with Blanderson. Was that how low I'd fallen? A teacher was my only friend?

And then, finally, the highlight of the day. Everyone was forced into the gym for the student body president debate. I had half a mind not to go at all, since Preethy was covering it anyway. But this was high school democracy, so you had to stand in line and file into the gym and sit quietly whether you were paying attention or not.

As I entered, I saw Preethy in the front row, hunched over a notebook. Serious looking. I felt sad for a moment, sad that I'd kind of written her off as not actually a serious journalist.

She wasn't flashy or edgy, but people trusted her. She wasn't the story. People knew she was fair. Meanwhile, I disliked both candidates equally, yet somehow everybody thought of me as the girl with a crush on Nolan Ramsey or as the troublemaker in the *New York Times*. I'd become the Beachside Strangler. I loped up to the top row of the bleachers, where all the most disengaged kids like to sit. I wanted to just slide into the background for a while.

On the gym floor, there was a simple podium and, about a dozen feet away, two chairs, one for Nolan and one for Jamie. Jamie sat stiff and confident. Nolan looked pretty much the way I'd look. Fidgety, slouchy, nervous, even when ninth graders started cheering, "*No-lan. No-lan.*" Seeing him squirm, I could imagine myself in his place, with everybody watching. And it kind of made me admire them both. It took some guts to do this.

Dr. Gordon took the stage first, standing next to the podium with a wireless mike.

"All right, everyone, listen up," he said. "Everyone, quiet. I'll wait. Quiet, everyone. Good. Welcome to this year's student body president debate. This is the moment you get to hear from the people who want to represent you, so I want you to listen closely and really think about what these two young people are saying. You know, you're all young men and women, taking on responsibilities of men and women, and voting is an important responsibility. So next week, I want you all to vote. People died for your right to vote. In Vietnam. In Iraq. At Selma. It's your duty as an American."

A couple of potheads sitting to my left giggled a bit at some unrelated joke.

"Quiet!" Gordon said. "Now, democracy is a conversation, and in conversation we have rules. What happened this morning in the parking lot—that's not an example of conversing within the rules. We're going to have a civil debate, which means no name-calling by the candidates, and everybody's going to be quiet while these two talk. You can cheer, but you are not allowed to boo. We will be civil."

"Moo?" said one of the potheads near me, in a normal speaking voice. Moo, not boo. I'm sure Gordon heard it. But it was him against all of us, and I guess he was picking his battles.

Gordon handed over the mike to Mr. Falkin, the new history teacher, who'd just gotten his graduate degree from Samford. Tall, skinny, bearded, with a soft voice. I'm inclined to call him a hipster, but after all my old-yearbook research, I realize Beachside High has always had at least one hairy-faced, earnest, noncoaching, intellectual male on staff. They last about two years, on average.

As soon as Gordon handed Falkin the mike, it stopped working. So we listened to him as he mumbled for a while, then swept his hand out toward the candidates as if expecting applause. A few kids in the front row clapped. Then more mumbles, some looking at note cards, and Nolan Ramsey came up to the podium. Big applause.

Mumble mumble mumble from Falkin. Nolan nodded.

"Okay, folks, I'm Nolan Ramsey," he said. "I've been asked to repeat all the questions because Mr. Falkin's microphone doesn't work. And the first question is to introduce yourself. I'm, uh, Nolan Ramsey? You all know me? I'm running for student body president." A few warm chuckles in the audience. Then: "I'm the *Republican* candidate for student body president." Big cheers, especially from Nolan's fist-pumping football friends. "And that's all you need to know about me."

More applause as Nolan headed back to his seat, passing Jamie on her way to the podium.

"The question, again, is simple," Jamie began. "Who are you, and why would you be the best student body president? I'm Jamie Scranton. A woman. An Alabamian. A Methodist. A journalist sometimes and a poet in my private time. When I get a chance to vote out there in the real world, I'll be a member of a political party. In here, in this building, I have no party. I want to work for you. I've already worked for you as editor of the school newspaper, as an organizer of the drive for tornado relief supplies, as an officer of the Beta Club. I want your permission to do more work for you. I want to be president for the entire student body. I'm Jamie Scranton."

Jamie started to leave, but Falkin mumbled something, and she stayed.

"All right," she said. "I've been asked to take the next question . . . and the question is . . . You know, I'm not sure I particularly like that question as it's phrased. I think it's based on something that was in the school newspaper that a lot of people have misinterpreted. Let me say this: we have excellent women's sports teams at this school. Volleyball, basketball, softball. In some cases, I won't name names, but the women's teams have gone to more playoffs in some sports than the men's. I can't figure out why we call them the Lady Bears when the boys are just the Bears. Why not Bears and Gentleman Bears? It's as if the boys are the mascot, and girls are just the mascot in a tutu."

I have thought the same thing many times. I also like the idea of the teams being She-Bears, a name that seems never to have occurred to the athletic boosters.

"I can't believe I'm saying this," Jamie continued, "but I was in fact misquoted in the press. I don't think I said that the band needs to come out twice as often for pep rallies. I didn't say anything about what the band's duties would be. I just said that if we celebrate the football team, we should celebrate the volleyball team in the same way."

My mind sort of melted. Jamie knew what she'd said in our interview, and I knew I'd reported it the way she said it. I had all the quotes right there in my notes. I'd transcribed them all from my recording and put stars by all the best stuff, just like Jamie had said a notetaker should do. Jamie was lying. I was already sitting alone at lunch, and now she was killing my reputation in front of the entire school. In a rage, I stood, my right hand clenched at my side in a fist. I don't know what I intended to do. A couple of people near me turned to look. Jamie saw me, made eye contact, and suddenly looked like a deer in headlights.

What are you doing, Lisa? I thought. And I sat back down, blushing.

"Wait a minute," Jamie said, holding up her hands. "Wait. Wait. . . . I have to rephrase something. . . . I'm not sure I was right to imply I was misquoted in the school newspaper. Maybe that came from somewhere else. From social media. I'm sorry for that. But my point remains. The volleyball team deserves equal attention." She shook her head like the girl who keeps hitting wrong notes at the piano recital. "I yield my time. I'm done."

Before she left the podium, Jamie turned her attention to her note cards, which she arranged nervously. She seemed to take a deep breath, then let it out in a sigh that ruined her posture. I could see every hope of the student body presidency draining out of her in that moment. Nolan didn't even look at her as she passed.

"The answer here is simple," he said at the podium. "Jamie is right. We have a great volleyball team. The Bears! And we should pay more attention to them. But, you know, there's another group out there that wins trophies and doesn't get nearly enough awards. And it has boys and girls in it. I'm talking about the band. Let's respect the mighty Bear band! If we want the volleyball team to get more attention, we should give it more attention, not ask someone to do that work for us. That's why I'm pledging to start going to volleyball games myself, every time my training schedule allows it. And I'm challenging all of the Bear football team to come with me to those games."

Applause. Then a senior in a football letter jacket stood and shouted, "*Bears!*" Which set off a brief wave of Bear chants. Finally Gordon stood and put his hands on his hips, and everything quieted down enough for Mr. Falkin to mumble another question.

"So, I should repeat the question?" Nolan said. "Okay, the question is that the editor of the student newspaper has been trying to get a chance to go watch a guy get executed. And what do I think of this? Is it the right thing to do?"

Oh, God, I thought. I realized I was blushing and, worse, genuinely nauseated. The whole school was about to hear a debate about *me* and *my* choices. And the whole thing wasn't about to go away. I was in over my head. I was drowning. And Nolan's long, frightened pause after repeating the question didn't make things any better.

"So," Nolan said. "I'll just admit I don't know anything about this. I'm too busy talking to the students, talking to you, to read newspapers. And let's just be honest: Who really likes newspapers?"

A cheer from the crowd. That seemed to give Nolan more confidence.

"So much of what you read in the papers out there is fake news," Nolan said to a louder cheer. "I find out about what's going on in school from my friends. I find out on Instagram. Teachers put stuff out there on Facebook so parents know what's going on. You can get it straight from the source without it having to be filtered through somebody's agenda. The way I see it—and perhaps I see it that way because I'm a proud *Republican*"—more cheers—"is that newspapers are a dying business. I don't know why we bother to teach people how to work in a dying business. I don't know why we'd want to put our name, the Beachside name, on some stunt like this. When you go to a football game, do you want kids from the other school to be like, 'That's Beachside, where they go watch executions?' That's weird."

Big cheers now. Nolan seemed to stand straighter. He finally knew what he was saying.

"My opponent may have a different opinion because not long ago she was editor of the paper," he said. "No, no booing. Dr. Gordon told us not to boo. No booing. Let's take action. Because I'm a Republican, and Republicans are men of action, I say we should go ahead and shut down the school newspaper entirely." Roars of applause. "And I'll do whatever I can, as student body president, to make that happen."

Nolan went back to his seat while the crowd continued to roar. Eventually Gordon had to stand up and stare at everybody angrily to get them to calm down. When Jamie came to the podium, it was so quiet you could hear her heels tap. They were offended taps, determined taps, taps that took no prisoners.

"Just to be clear," she said, "I'd like you to repeat the question."

This time, everybody leaned forward to hear Mr. Falkin mumble the question. Which was totally drowned out by the sound of four hundred kids shifting in their seats. A couple of nervous coughs.

"Okay," Jamie said, studiously shifting papers on the podium. "So the question, the exact question, is: Do I think it was a good idea for Lisa Rives—and that's the proper pronunciation of her name, *Reeves*—was it the right thing for her to ask for permission to witness an execution on behalf of the *Beachside Bulletin*? Obviously, this has special meaning for me because I am indeed the former editor. So if you ask me if it's the right choice, to seek to watch the execution, I'd have to say my answer is no."

A light dusting of applause.

"Let me be clear about one thing," Jamie said. "If a local newspaper is guaranteed a seat at an execution, then I think Lisa is correct that the *Beachside Bulletin* has a *right* to be there. Because no matter what some people out there think, a student newspaper *is* a real newspaper. Because you are real. Your lives are real. If a pep rally is on the front page of the paper, and a pep rally is the biggest thing that happened in school that week, so be it. What's important inside these walls, that's news, because you're a community, and you deserve to know. And let's not get into Facebook as a news source. How many times did people stay out of school last year because of Facebook rumors about meningitis outbreaks or school-shooting threats? And how many turned out to be true? None? One case of tuberculosis in a kid who was diagnosed over the summer and never actually showed up here? We, the *Beachside Bulletin*, we told you the truth. The boring but *true* truth."

Jamie was getting worked up. But I could see she was losing

the crowd. Only the Blandersons of the world get teary eyed about a passionate defense of boringness.

"What Lisa's doing isn't fake news," Jamie said. "It's smart. It's aggressive. It's also not really the core mission of the paper. This is a publication about *us*, about *our* lives. Just because you have a right to view an execution doesn't mean you should."

The applause picked up a little.

"And let me tell you something," Jamie continued. "I am a *woman* of action. Democratic, Republican, there are *women* all around you who are *women* of action." Cheers, mostly from girls. "And when women take action, we do it firmly but with love in our hearts and wisdom in our minds. My opponent calls himself a conservative, but he wants to shut down an institution that's been here since before we were born. We don't need to kill our newspaper. We need a new editor!"

Applause, loud applause. My nausea at this point gave way to anger. I was so angry I don't even remember if there were more questions. I don't remember Dr. Gordon telling us all to go back to class, and I don't remember descending the bleachers—something that normally sticks in my mind after pep rallies because of the vertigo I feel every time I climb down those bleacher seats. There's so far to fall that it's a fall that could actually break an arm or some teeth. And then there's the knowledge that when you got up, with your broken teeth and bloody mouth, the whole school would be there to look at you in pity or to laugh. You'd become That Girl Who Fell, a social status so low that most schools don't even have it.

What I do remember is standing on the gym floor as students streamed by. I remember just standing there watching Jamie as she collected her papers and put them in her impeccable little folders and slid them into her backpack. I stood about twenty feet away, like a first grader on the playground who wants to be asked to come and play. But I was in no mood to play.

Jamie glanced up for a moment and our eyes met. She looked, I don't know, *scared* of me. I shook my head and headed for the door. When I was about halfway there I felt a soft, warm hand on my shoulder.

"Preethy," I said, turning. But it wasn't Preethy. It was Jamie.

"Lisa," she said. "I understand that you're upset with me. I believe in transparency. Let's talk. Tell me what you're thinking right now."

I lifted a finger, as if I was about to start a tirade, then noticed the amused stares of kids walking past. I put my hand back down.

"I'm not going to discuss it here, Jamie," I said. "I'm not interested in having a conversation, or a conflict, right here in front of everybody."

"Don't kid yourself," Jamie said. "Every conflict in this school is in front of everybody. All conflicts are in public, in the end."

I looked up to the ceiling in anger. My hand kept trying to rise, as if to point at her, but I knew how that would look.

"You know damn well what I'm mad about," I said. "You aren't showing any solidarity. Free speech, editorial freedom— it's okay as long as *you're* the editor. But you won't stand up for it for anybody else."

"I'm sorry you feel that way, Lisa," she said. "I just don't think you're ready to be editor. You've clearly got trouble keeping your emotions and your opinions under control."

"Oh, don't give me that," I said. "I'm only the editor because you left. You're the one who couldn't resist injecting yourself into politics."

"You're a loose cannon," Jamie said. "I know about the *Beachside Strangler*. You're turning the paper into something that just serves your morbid curiosity. It's not about the school anymore."

I flushed deep red. Only after meeting Rhee Ann and having my name in newspapers across the country did I really understand what a bonehead move the *Strangler* idea would have been. Blanderson had been right about that. She'd been kind. But Jamie wasn't Blanderson. I was tired of her acting like she was my teacher.

"I've got my faults," I said. "I've made mistakes. But you know what? I'm *twice* the editor you ever were. There, I said it. I've got curiosity and I've got guts. I ask the questions that I want answers to. How did you cover the last presidential election? A photo of each candidate, a list of clubs they're in, a questionnaire? People *know* what this election is about. They're going to vote. They care."

"You made it partisan," she said. "You turned some blue-skying about pep rallies into a battle between me and the band."

I rolled my eyes. Lisa, don't let your hand rise above waist level.

"Oh, for crying out loud," I said. "Democrats! If you're going to be one, just be one. If you've got a policy, just stand by it. Don't blame me if people don't like it. At least they know what the policy is."

"But the other guy doesn't even have policies—except for getting rid of you," Jamie said. "And people prefer that. They prefer that to good leadership."

"Not my problem," I said. And then my hands did come up, in a shrug. "I don't tell people how to vote. I couldn't make them vote the way I wanted if I tried. Not my job."

Jamie lifted her finger then. *Jamie* pointed.

"Let me just say this," she said. "I've kept this to myself for a long time, but after today I'm breaking my silence. I think you're a bully. When you stood up in the bleachers, I felt threatened. I feel threatened now."

My dad once said that laughter is the body's natural response to absurdity. He told me this after Mom came to us upset about an old news article on her iPad, an article about people who laughed when they first heard news of September 11 and who felt guilty about it later. Dad said humor is only part of laughter. If the full moon suddenly winked out of existence, if the president split in two on national TV, revealing an alien behind a rubber mask, you'd laugh.

And that's what I did. I barked a little laugh, then swallowed the rest because I realized what was going on. Even laughter looks bad when you're being accused of bullying.

"You know," I said, "I believe it's you who came to me. You who wanted this conversation. You who said all conflicts are public. You're seeking public office, and I'm the press, and you just said you felt threatened because I literally *stood up* to you. And enough of this 'breaking my silence' crap. You're talking to a human being, not shouting on Twitter."

Jamie was speechless for a second. If I were the kind of person who seeks out these battles, I would have twisted that moment into a ring and worn it for years. Instead, I just turned around and left, shaking my head. I knew who'd really lost the fight—I could tell by the stares and the whispers as I made my way through the halls. Arguing like that with Jamie in front of everybody was the equivalent of falling down the bleachers. I was walking around with blood on my face, and there was no school nurse to fix me, no excuse to get me out of school for the rest of the day.

How did Jamie know about the *Beachside Strangler*? I wondered For a moment, I was mad at Blanderson. I even entertained a little conspiracy theory about Gordon surveilling Blanderson's office via the intercom and sharing that info with Jamie. But then came the sick realization that, honestly, I had known how Jamie knew out all along.

I found Preethy just as the halls were beginning to clear out. She was at her locker. At our lockers. It seemed like years ago that we'd stood in line together at orientation and begged for lockers that were side by side, even if it meant we had to be on the bottom row.

"Hey, Preeth," I said, kind of weakly. "How do you think it went?"

"Okay, I guess," she said, closing her locker. "Bell's about to ring."

"Preethy, can we talk?" I said. "I have an important question."

"Got to get to class," she said. "We're almost late."

She turned to leave. I raised my voice so she could hear me.

"I'm Wonder Woman," I said. "Remember when we used to play that?"

She turned and saw me, hand in the air, twirling my lasso. A sad smile.

"I can't do this now, Lisa," she said. "The bell's about to ring."

I tossed my lasso. The bell rang. Preethy shook her head as the last few kids ran to class. But she didn't leave. I mimed reeling in a rope. She waddled toward me, hands at her sides, as if bound.

"I've got you in my golden lasso now," I said. "You've got to tell me the truth."

For a brief moment, I could smell a whiff of suntan oil, see wet Barbies fighting on water-stained pavement. We hadn't played this game in a long time. And I could see Preethy was thinking that too.

"You've got to tell me the truth, no matter what," I said. "Did you tell Jamie about the *Beachside Strangler*?"

"Yes," she said.

"Who's a better newspaper editor?" I asked. "Me or Jamie?"

"You are," she said. "You're too good. You're so good it's scary. Literally scary."

Her answer came so quick that I knew she didn't even mind admitting it.

"Who would you rather work for, me or Jamie?" I asked.

"Jamie," she said. Another quick answer.

Now I was scared. Telling the truth is scary. Getting the truth is scary too. But I had to know.

"Preethy, are we still friends?" I asked.

"I . . . I don't know," she said. "I don't think so."

I hope I looked as hurt as I felt.

"Why?" I asked. "Why are we not still friends?"

She sighed.

"I think," she said. "I think . . . the thing that makes you a better editor than Jamie is the thing I don't like. I'm your sidekick. I'm not Jamie's sidekick."

"Are we breaking up?" I asked. "For real?"

She started to cry.

"Yes," she said. "Yes, we are."

She didn't even reach up to wipe her nose, because her hands were tied. With tears in my eyes, I waved my lasso hand in a circle.

"There, you're free," I said. "I'm letting you go, my love. You'll never be in my lasso again."

Then, weirdly, we hugged. Preethy didn't head for class. She bolted for the bathroom. I ran downstairs, past a dumbfounded coach, wiping my eyes. I had to find a different girl's room.

That's my life. Preethy and I don't even cry in the same bathroom anymore.

Genius

I won the election, I guess. And I lost high school.

Of course, Nolan Ramsey got the most votes. About two-thirds of the votes. I'd expected, with all the debate and the cheering and the hating on Lisa, that there would have been a high turnout. But when the count was done, there were only five more votes cast this year than last year.

"It's America," Blanderson said. "Even when we care about elections, we don't care about elections."

A week later, everyone but Jamie Scranton had forgotten about the whole thing. Even Nolan Ramsey forgot. He was late to the first student-council meeting because he lost track of the time. But soon he settled into the time-honored council tradition of not doing anything, really. The council voted to sell spirit ribbons again next year. The council voted to again spend the proceeds on the homecoming dance. There was no resolution to shut down the school newspaper. That would take work, and anyway, no one seemed to care if he didn't fulfill his promise.

"I still think it's a good idea to keep our heads down for a bit," Blanderson said. "I know we're supposed to write without fear or favor. But we've already produced more editions than most papers at schools this size will do in a year. And this last issue—with the election coverage and the death-penalty story—is literally the best issue of a high school newspaper I've ever seen. We could stop right here, for the year, and we'd be ahead of the game."

I wanted to nod. But I'm Lisa, the one who wants to know the whole truth even when it's ugly. Even when I've had all I can take.

"Go back to that 'without fear or favor' thing," I said. "If we're tired, if we're trying to save the paper from being canceled, if we've got a paper we can submit for awards and we don't want to mess it up, how is that not fear?"

Blanderson threw her hands up.

"You've got me there," she said. "Maybe I'm a hypocrite. But I do think it's a good idea to pick your battles. Football season is almost over. Nothing much happens during the holidays. We're in a lawsuit against the Department of Corrections, and people call me every day wanting an interview with you. I think we should use this time to make sure we get the execution coverage right. That doesn't happen until next semester. We can take our time and have an even better issue than this one. This effing *amazing* issue."

I heard all of that, but at the same time, I didn't really hear it at all.

"So," I said. "People are still calling about interviews?"

That's what I mean when I say I won the election. That election-day issue of the *Beachside Bulletin*—with the Rhee Ann interview and my editorial about why I was trying to get in to see the execution—made me a star in the small world where Blanderson, apparently, spends a lot of her mental time. The *Columbia Journalism Review* asked me for an interview. The Poynter Institute, which apparently is a big deal in journalism, did a blog post about our lawsuit. Blanderson kept saying: "The goal is to get the story, not *be* the story." But I could tell she was proud that the *Bulletin* was getting all this interest. We weren't even trying to win Twitter or get our name on other people's front pages, but we were succeeding anyway.

"People are still calling," Blanderson said. "It's dying down a little bit. The last few calls were from education magazines, mostly. Anyway, I think we need to plan how to handle this. Like I always say, we're not supposed to be the story. We need to start thinking about how we'll cover the execution, assuming we get in. What kind of psychological preparation do you need to be able to do something like this? Can we convince Gordon to give you an excused absence since it's on a weekday? I think we should talk to some people who've witnessed executions, to see what we can expect."

"Frankly," I said, "I don't even know how I'm going to get down there. My mom refuses to take me. My dad can't take me, because he's going on a trip with his, his assistant that same week."

I didn't mean to trip up on "his assistant." Why would I mention Denise at all? I realized suddenly just how long she'd been living rent-free in my mind. On the rare occasions when all the noise about Preethy or the election died down, Denise was always there to bother me. In my mental hallway lined with family pictures, Denise was there in the frame beside Dad. Denise with the already-perfect life, creeping on the only man I'd ever really trusted. Denise who could ruin Thanksgiving and Christmas forever.

Blanderson noticed my "assistant" flub. She looked at me for a long moment.

"I don't want to pry, but is everything okay at home?" she said.

"Everything is okay," I said. "Everything at home is just okay. It's always been just okay. I'm well fed. Nobody abuses me. I guess we're rich. My mom is always pushing me to buy better clothes and to want more stuff. My dad may have a girlfriend. I guess that bothers me. I don't know why it bothers me. He's always spent half the week in another town. Why should I care if he has a girlfriend there?"

Blanderson said nothing.

"I mean, should I care?" I said.

"Sounds like you do care," she said. "I think it's probably okay to care. I mean, it's *your* family. It's okay not to care. He's not your husband. So, the bad news is that you can't really choose whether to care or not. Your body decides for you, sort of. The good news is, there's no wrong answer. I think you've got a right to feel about it any way you want to feel."

I nodded. I was listening. I was listening to every word. But I was looking at the whiteboard, not at her. Thinking hard.

"Is there anything else?" she said. "You seem so sad lately. It makes me think maybe there's more."

I laughed. "Isn't that enough?"

"For some people, maybe," she said. "I kind of doubt that's enough to sink you. You know, there's a theory called 'good-enough parenting.' It's this idea that most people come out pretty well if they're just fed and clothed and educated and treated with basic decency as kids. You don't have to play Mozart for them in the cradle to get them to live up to their potential. You just have to do the basics."

"So," I said, "you're saying that having two parents who are faithful to each other is the equivalent of having Mozart played to you in the cradle."

Blanderson shrugged. "Maybe, yeah."

Still staring at the whiteboard.

"Maybe there is something," I said, waving my arm broadly. "This. All this. High school. It's a crappy arrangement to begin with. And it's even harder now that I'm Fake News Lisa. Do you realize I don't talk to anybody my age anymore? Preethy's gone. I talk to you. I talk to the Educational Press Law Center lawyers. I talk to reporters who want to write about the execution. Did you know the other day I cried on the phone with a recruiter from the University of Missouri? Something she said about how I'd really fit in at their journalism school."

"I'm sorry this is happening to you," Blanderson said. "Maybe I should have warned you. Maybe I assumed everybody knew. This is the life of a journalist. You lose a lot of friends. You lose a lot of connections. I remember one time our Girl Scout troop was looking for help raising money, and they created this committee of community big shots to go out and ask other big shots for money. And they invited my dad to join the group and make calls. And he raised almost no money. The other guys on the committee were like, 'But the governor knows you by name, and you have a Rolodex full of elected officials.' But he couldn't call any of those people and ask them for a favor, not even on behalf of an organization. It wouldn't be ethical. And soon all the parents in the troop, which was really the only group he was part of, all of them pretty much thought he was a slacker and a fraud. That's the life. Independence. Necessary but overrated."

"I've had my own run-ins with the Girl Scouts. 'God and my country,'" I said, making air quotes.

"Dad was fine with God and his country," Blanderson said. "A veteran. A very conservative, defense-minded Democrat, when he dared to share a political view. Didn't win him any friends. But let's look on the bright side. Mizzou is trying to recruit you to their journalism school! Do you realize how great that is? The University of Missouri is maybe the best J-school in the country. You've already caught their eye. At fifteen!"

I sighed.

"Maybe I'm a 'young genius.'" Again, I made air quotes, but Blanderson still looked appalled. "No, I don't mean it in an arrogant way. I've been reading this book, where a sociologist studies all these people who've achieved great success in their teens. It's depressing. It's awful. These kids who get a PhD at fourteen or publish a novel at thirteen—almost all of them wind up accomplishing nothing after that. A freak as a kid and a nobody as an adult. I'm starting to think I'm going to land in that category too. Maybe this execution is the only thing I'll ever write."

I was fishing for reassurance. But the thing I like most about Blanderson is that she's honest.

"Well, if this is the pinnacle of your career," she said, "we'd better make sure we do it right."

Ever say something, something you didn't know was stupid or shallow, and then see that look on somebody's face? Ever lie awake at night thinking about something you said years ago, something really dumb, and then suddenly blush, in the dark, alone?

I did. I did it again and again after I told Blanderson that maybe I was a young genius. Did she think I sat around thinking of myself as a genius all the time? I didn't, or at least I didn't think I did. But, hey, I read a whole book about child geniuses. Why would I do that if I wasn't a little full of myself? Okay, a lot full of myself.

These questions are so hard to answer in the dark. When you're lying awake at 2:00 a.m. When the screen of your phone is a shard of white light in your eye.

She picked up on the second ring. A gummy, sleepy voice. "H'lo?"

I could picture her in her room, warm under a fluffy comforter on that chilly night, wearing her fuzzy duck socks, a pile of manga beside her.

"Preethy, it's me," I said. "Lisa."

"I know," she said.

"I'm sorry I woke you up," I said. "I just want to say I'm sorry."

"Sorry for what?" she said. "You don't have anything to be sorry for."

"You were right," I said. "About being a sidekick. I've been really arrogant. I've let this job go to my head. I'm not calling you to ask for anything or to win you back. Although that would be nice. I just genuinely want you to know I'm sorry. I'm sorry I hurt you."

Preethy moaned a little. She still didn't seem quite awake.

"You don't have anything to be sorry for," she said again. "I'm not hurt."

"Then why?" I asked. I didn't have to say more.

I could hear a rustle as she sat up.

"Lisa, I already live with one person who . . . I don't know," she said. "It's like you're turning into my dad. He's smart and he's right, and he can't let it go. He's always in people's faces with the details. I'm not like that. You know I don't do conflict. I don't like conflict."

I sort of held my breath. I was worried that she was going to ask me not to cover the execution. I was worried that if she did, I would say yes.

"What should I do?" I said.

"Nothing," she said. "Nothing different than what you're doing. You're like my dad. That's just who you are. Don't back away from the execution. I'm proud of you. Really. But I'm just not comfortable going some of the places you go. We're becoming very different people, I think."

"I love you," I said. "You're my only . . . I don't know. I don't have a sister, or any cousins. There's only you."

"Lisa," she said. And then nothing followed.

"After the execution, I'll step back," I said. "Things will go back to normal. We'll spend the summer watching anime together, like old times."

"That sounds nice," she said. "But do you really believe that? Do you really think you're going to go and watch someone get killed and write a story about it that everybody reads, and then you'll just come back, and we'll paint stickmen on the driveway with water, like we're ten-year-olds? I'd like that. I want to go back. But I don't think that's going to happen."

"See? You want it too," I said. "We can go back."

Preethy seemed perturbed.

"Lisa, it's two in the morning," she said. "I'm supposed to be dreaming. A time of day when you just see and feel and don't have to think. And you're calling me up and wanting answers. You want to know whether we can go back to being kids again. Do you just want me to say it? That we can't go back? When you know I want that more than anything else in the world? Why do you always have to force these things? Why do you always have to have answers? It's two in the morning."

I don't even recall how the conversation ended. And when it did, I wanted to punch myself in the face. Yeah, Lisa, you're a genius all right. You just called another girl and told her you love her. You just admitted you don't have any friends. What would happen if Preethy blabbed to someone about this the next day at school? I knew she probably wouldn't. It wasn't like her. But if she did, I'd spend the rest of my high school career as a scorned woman, supposedly pining over Nolan and Preethy both.

So, not a genius move. For the record, I don't believe in geniuses. I simply needed a word for what was happening to me. A model to work from. What was the name for this? When you're doing something right and smart and nobody understands you? When people see you coming, and they have that look in their eye—respect, suspicion, and fear all at once? Tell me, what do you call that?

Thanksgiving came and went. Mom and I went to Chattanooga to shop for Dad's Christmas presents, though I knew it was really a ploy to get me to try on clothes. If I were the daughter she wanted, I'd have bought all my winter stuff in summer. Since I'm me, I avoid the whole thing until it actually gets cold and hoodies no longer stop the shivers. Winter shopping isn't so bad, though. A season of dark colors, long functional padded coats—stuff Mom and I can agree on. Try on everything she wants you to try, and then put the girly pearl-colored scarves and white toboggans in the drawer, never to be seen again.

Things were good that day. My court case had been filed and was sitting on some judge's desk under a stack of other cases. The folks at Educational Press Law Center had told me not to expect a ruling before January, probably just days before the execution. On the car ride home, the Christmas station was on the radio, and I was nestled inside a coat and gloves, feeling armored and safe. Mom was driving, and she wasn't even bugging me about when I'm going to get my permit, so I could watch the landscape and daydream like a kid. Right then, life was good.

My phone buzzed in my pocket.

"Lisa, it's Lew East, at the Minden paper? Can we talk a little bit, reporter to reporter? Off the record."

"Go," I said. Lew always sounded strangely brusque, like a western-movie tough guy, but with that high-pitched voice that made his brusqueness sound comical. I can be brusque too.

"So, I wanted to let you know that we, in Minden, plan to file an amicus brief in your case," he said. "On your side, of course. I talked a long time with my editors, and we finally came to the decision that it was important to support your claim over the other intervenors'."

Okay, some background. An intervenor is somebody who files a legal brief in somebody else's court case. There are two parties in a case, and an intervenor is a third person who steps in. So, like, if the governor gets divorced and a newspaper steps in to ask the court to make those divorce records public, they'd be an intervenor. An amicus brief is something you file in support of one side or the other, even if you're not part of the case.

"I don't understand," I said. "I don't know about any other intervenors. What are you talking about?"

Lew chuckled.

"I thought your lawyers would have told you," he said. "*Birmingham Buzz* just filed a court brief saying that they are entitled to the local-newspaper seat at the execution. Not you."

"What?" I almost shouted. "They're not a local newspaper. They're in Jefferson County!"

"They're claiming that because they distribute their paper in Beachside, they're the local paper," Lew said. "Here in Minden, we deliver both our paper and their paper. They send the papers here, and we send them out on the route with our drivers. But for distribution in Beachside, precisely because there's no local paper, they have their own distribution center in Oconostota. They say that shows they're doing business in Beachside."

"Oconostota isn't even in the same county!" I said.

"I know," Lew said. "It's complete BS. I guess the question is whether a judge will get that. Small-town life is tough when you're competing with the big dogs. When I hear other news outlets say Minden is 'in the Birmingham area,' I just want to tear my hair out."

Nobody reacted to the news in the way I expected. I thought Mom would gloat. Finally, here was something that could end her daughter's ridiculous quest to see a man die. Instead, she just listened and nodded as I explained what had happened.

"Oconostota?" she said with a look of disgust. "That's almost offensive. *Birmingham Buzz* isn't a local business. Name one person in Beachside who actually gets the paper version of the *Buzz* delivered. You can get it for free online!"

Blanderson, the next day, wasn't fired up the way I was.

"This might be the end of the road for us," she said.

This was after school, during one of the newspaper planning sessions that had become my favorite part of the week—my substitute for unloading with Preethy.

"I don't see how you can say that," I said. "Their argument is garbage. We're much more of a local newspaper than they are."

"I don't know," Blanderson said. "Judges don't like to shake things up. And you present them with some tough choices. Should a kid be allowed to go into an execution chamber? In a world where everybody's screaming on the internet, who's a journalist and what's a newspaper? We have a good case, but if

Birmingham Buzz steps in, that gives the judge an easy out. On the bright side, maybe if we push it, we can actually get *Buzz* to open a bureau here. That would be progress."

I scoffed. "A bureau? You mean some part-timer who works from home, covering the county commission? They call it a bureau, like it's a local office, but it's just one underpaid reporter. You're the one who taught me that."

"A reporter who would probably live in Oconostota too," Blanderson said. "But that would mean more county coverage than we've been getting. So maybe this is our legacy. We push *Buzz*—and maybe even some other papers—to step into the market to compete with us. Maybe if they win, you could even apply to be the bureau."

I stood.

"I can't believe you!" I said. "*This* is the Beachside newspaper. *We* are local. *We are a real newspaper.*"

"You're right," she said. "You're right, and you make me proud. You've made this a real newspaper. Now we have real newspaper problems. Real courts. Real competition. Real, tough choices."

Just then the intercom barked to life. Why do schools still have intercoms, when everybody has a phone in their pocket? My guess: authoritarians love loudspeakers.

"Ms. Blandings-Sanderson," said Gordon's voice, dripping with anger. "Please come up here to the office, and tell me why there are television reporters in my school parking lot again."

Blanderson sighed, pressed the Reply button. "On my way," she said. I picked up my backpack. "Lisa, you don't have to go," Blanderson said. "I'll talk to him about this."

"Oh, I'm not going to the office," I said. "You go to the office. I'm going to the parking lot."

"No, Lisa, I don't think that's wise. Shouldn't we prep before doing an interview?"

"You're on your way to the office," I said. "And school is over. So I'm leaving the building."

I left before she could say more.

"Yes," I said, leaning toward the microphone. "L-I-S-A R-I-V-E-S. Pronounced *Reeves*. I'm the editor of the *Beachside Bulletin*."

There were only three reporters, one from a TV station and two from local radio stations. But with the camera and sound guys plus the big vans wrapped in ads for their stations, it looked like a full-on press conference.

The TV reporter went first.

"So tell me: Why do you want to see someone be executed?" she asked. "And why should the state let someone so young go into the execution chamber?"

The toughest question. I took a deep breath.

"I'll take that second question first," I said. "South Carolina executed a fourteen-year-old. They strapped a kid named George Stinney into the electric chair and killed him. Clearly South Carolina didn't have a problem putting a kid in the chamber then."

"That's South Carolina, not here," a radio reporter said.

"True, but it gets to my point," I said. "Alabama might have executed someone my age, or even younger, at some point. It was certainly legal back in the twentieth century. I've tried to find out. And I can't. Before 1927, when Alabama's electric chair was created, nobody really kept a complete record of who was executed and why. They'd build a gallows right there at the local jail and hang them. From then until the 1970s, even the state records are pretty spotty. All we can know about some of those executions is what newspapers tell us. If the press isn't there, then it's a black hole. Some people just want to shrug and go on, but I want to know the truth. Even if it's unpleasant."

"Why you, though?" asked the TV reporter. "*Birmingham Buzz* is a real newspaper, with a long history. Their coverage will be read by people all over this county. Why shouldn't they have the seat at the execution?"

I bristled.

"I'm a real newspaper!" I said. "I mean, the *Beachside Bulletin* is a real newspaper. I'm a real journalist. We live here. Who's talked to the victim's family? Who's going to be here after the execution, still reporting on Beachside?"

The other radio guy said, "You say you're the newspaper—"

"A slip of the tongue," I said.

"But it does bring up an important issue," he said. "As journalists, our role is to tell the story, not to be the story. Yet your name has been in the headlines about this fairly often. You're here talking to us now. What would you say to critics who say this is a young student's attempt to make a name for herself?"

I blanked for a moment. All I could think of just then were the words "Beachside Strangler."

"Here's the thing," I said. "If I'm an unusual journalist, if I'm a curiosity, then I am one because the state of Alabama made me one. They're the ones who are saying I'm different from other reporters. They're putting the spotlight on me. My job is to fight for access to information, whether I'm in the spotlight or not."

I could hear distant shouting behind me. Gordon coming down the hill.

"Is it fair to say this fight has made you famous in some circles?" one of the radio guys asked. "What's it like being famous in high school?"

I got a sinking feeling. If I wasn't famous already, I would be now. Famous for trying to be famous.

"This whole thing is the worst thing that's happened in my entire life," I said. "Maybe I'm kind of sheltered, but I can't think of anything, for me, that's been this bad. I've lost friends. My grades are dropping. I'm pretty sure everybody in school is mad at me."

Gordon's shouts were closer. He was barking my name and ordering me to "come here." I gave the reporters a fake smile.

"That's all I have time for," I said. "Thanks!"

If you're going to get suspended, do it just before the holidays. In most classes, I didn't miss anything except make-work. Three days was just long enough to miss all the movies Coach Jones was showing in history class, full of Civil War generals with obviously fake beards. But I did lose the chance to submit a big project in science, and I missed a huge test in Blanderson's class that I could have aced in my sleep. So in one of my favorite classes, the only class where I was really a star, I suddenly fell from the top of the class to near the bottom. I'd wind up with a C in journalism. With all my victories and failures, just average overall.

One big problem with suspension: being stuck at home with Mom for three days with little buffer between us. The first day wasn't so bad. Mom went into town on "business," whatever business is for someone who retired early. I think she was as uncomfortable with me entering her mom space as I was with her being around.

The next day was worse. Daytime television, as you may

know, is awful, and when it's not baseball season, daytime TV is Mom's video wallpaper. News shows that switch from starving refugees to the latest cooking trend in the blink of an eye. That show where a panel of celebrity women argue about the news, followed by another show with another panel of celebrities. I couldn't complain, though. Mom was quiet and a bit gruff, essentially ignoring me as if the suspension had never happened. I didn't want to call attention to myself.

Then, a little before lunch, came the text. I didn't have Lew East in my contacts, but I knew from the number it was him.

> Just heard about the court's ruling. That's a shame.
> I was looking forward to meeting you at the prison.

I stood there in the kitchen furiously texting Blanderson and the Educational Press lawyers, then I finally found it in the "breaking news" feed from *Birmingham Buzz*. The court had ruled that *Birmingham Buzz* was the local newspaper for Beachside. They'd have an automatic seat at Houser's execution and at any future execution for a crime committed in Beachside. I was shut out.

I wasn't even upset about it. I was done. I'd lost my only friend, I was suspended from school, and now the court had confirmed what so many of the grown-ups in my life had been telling me: the *Beachside Bulletin* wasn't a real newspaper. I didn't say anything to Mom. I just went out and sat on the deck, looking at the lake. I didn't think I looked upset, but I guess I must have slammed the door a bit hard because soon Mom came out and sat down beside me.

"So you must have found out about the court case," Mom said.

"You knew?"

She held up her tablet.

"Just now," she said. "I've got a Google News alert on you."

Quiet for a moment. Then she spoke again. "So, are you okay?"

"I've reached a place of deep not caring," I said. "I just go through all this stuff, the newspaper and the court case and all, as if I cared. But inside I'm numb."

Mom nodded and looked at the lake.

"Maybe this newspaper thing, maybe this execution stuff, is a good thing after all," she said. "It's good to get a taste of that experience early on. That place of not caring—that's a place you'll go back to again and again."

I didn't know if she was joking. I turned my head to her with a look that said as much.

"No, I'm serious," she said. "There will be moments when numbness will get you through. You'll be so exasperated, you'll feel like you don't even know your name. And the best thing to do, usually, is exactly what was already your plan. Over there across the lake? I sold that house. One of the buyers— well, potential buyers—was a couple who loved the house but said all kinds of demeaning things about the community. The locals. My community, me. The wife was nice otherwise. The husband was chatty, with a little lilt in his voice, the way men are when they want to flirt. And as soon as I was alone in one of the rooms with him, he basically hit on me. Grabbed my hand, just my hand, and I think he was moving in to kiss me, and I had to kind of dodge. With his wife in the other room. What a jerk! And the whole time, all I could think about was me—not her but me. What if she walks in and sees him forcing a kiss on me, and she gets mad and goes out and ruins my name in the profession? What if she tells a story that gets back to your father? I wanted to shoot the guy."

"And you didn't?" I said. "You've always seemed like the shooting type, more so than Dad."

"No, honey, I didn't, because I had a job to do," she said. "I went to that cold place you're in right now. Left the room, did the whole showing as if nothing had happened. And of course they weren't the ones who ended up buying the house, and I can just picture the conversation on the way home. She says I was kind of cold. He says he was trying to bring me out of my shell. She says she thought he was flirting, and he says: You know, I think she actually liked me in that way, but you know frizzy redheads aren't my type. I'm out an afternoon and out a client, and I'm just some bit player in the screenplay of their lives. And stuff like that happened every week. But I kept going. And eventually I made enough money to retire. Not everybody gets to say, 'I sold it all. I'm going to the house.' Some people have to keep on going back to the cold place again and again. It's good to be wealthy."

I shook my head. "I don't think of us as wealthy," I said. "I always thought we were more like upper-middle class."

"Well, I know *I've* been wealthy," she said. "There hasn't been a day of my life that I haven't owned real estate. And then I turned that into a job. When owning things is your job, you're wealthy."

"A genuine capitalist," I said. "Shouldn't you be out oppressing people?"

She patted my knee.

"Sweetie, I retired just so I could stay home and oppress you," she said. "The most important person in my life."

Things were quiet and warm for a moment. Sometimes I like my mom. I like it when we're being honest without meanness.

"You know," I said, "I don't know how to say this, but maybe you should spend a little more time oppressing that other person in your life. Maybe he needs to be less free. In one way."

"Why, whatever do you mean?" she said with a Scarlett O'Hara coyness. "I can't imagine what you're talking about."

I turned to face her directly, taking a deep breath. It was time. "Mom, we have to talk about Denise."

She got a strange twinkle in her eye. "What about Denise?"

"She calls here all the time," I said. "Dad is over there half the week, with her. He's going to Las Vegas with her, for goodness' sake. And she's young and pretty, and she's into all the dumb science stuff that Dad is into. I know you think they're having an affair. I hear little hints all the time."

Mom laughed.

"Good," she said. "I'm glad you think that. I'm glad you think I'm thinking that. I hope that's what your dad thinks too."

I shook my head. "I don't get you sometimes."

Mom gave me a little side hug.

"Honey, I guess I should have told you before," she said. "Denise is a spy."

I pushed her back. Just what I needed right then was to find out that one or both of my parents were committing espionage.

"What?" I said. "You've got to be kidding me! What the hell is going on?"

"Not a spy for another government," Mom said. "She's a spy for me."

I opened my mouth, but no words came out.

"Look," Mom said. "Men are a great thing. I mean, if men are what you turn out to be interested in, you'll find that a man, for all his failings, is exactly what you need sometimes. I mean, he's exactly what you sometimes need."

"Ew," I said.

"Look, I give your dad a lot of grief, but I know what he is. He's a fine man, smart and fit and sexy. You can love men. You can even trust them sometimes. But you can only trust them so far, if you're wise. You need to keep them in line. You need to check in on them."

I stayed silent.

"So," Mom continued, "the moment your dad got this job—away from home for half the week, working in some top-secret vault with a hot young assistant—I knew what I had to do. What would any smart woman do? I mean, you think it out."

"Make friends with the assistant," I said. "Because it's a lot harder to cheat with a friend's husband, I guess."

"Something like that," Mom said. "Actually, we are friends now. But at first it was more . . . transactional. I called her and said that I was the wife and I didn't like my husband living in so much secrecy, and I basically ordered her to report on my husband for me. I wanted to know what he did in his spare time and who he was hanging out with. And she totally got it. She's kind of French, you know."

"But she's always calling and asking to speak to Dad," I said.

"Of course she's asking for Dad," Mom said. "When *you* answer. It wouldn't do for her to call and ask for me, would it? And it's not like she doesn't have his cell number."

Mind blown. "So that's why she's always calling the landline, because it's—"

"*My* phone in *my* kitchen," she said. "Which is *my* room in the house when you aren't messing in it."

"But I caught Dad creeping on her on Facebook," I said.

Mom seemed genuinely surprised. "Really?"

"Well, I didn't catch Dad," I said. "I got up one morning, and the laptop was open, and it was on her page."

Mom chuckled.

"That was almost certainly me," she said. "But maybe not. Maybe in some weak moments, he looks at a photo of his way-too-young assistant and has a little fantasy. If so, I'm not too worried about it, because *she's* definitely not interested. But I bet it was my Facebook. At one point she was giving me daily reports."

"Reports on what? What's he doing?" I asked.

"Nothing, I'm happy to say," Mom said. "Your dad is an overgrown adolescent. Whenever he travels, he makes sure he gets a hotel room with a video game console and a fitness center. He games all night, and he runs in the morning."

I laughed. "Video games? Dad? The guy who's always lecturing me about less screen time?"

"The same," Mom said. "Look, he's alone and free. He has a few hours a day to live like a bachelor. He could be going to strip clubs or taking off his ring and going to bars, but this is his addiction instead. He doesn't go out and have drinks with coworkers or do poker nights or anything. He's even embezzling from me to feed his addiction. When he travels, he gets the per diem in cash so he can buy video games without me seeing the purchase on his card. Denise says it's about fifty percent of what he talks about: video games."

"I can't believe it," I said. "Dad exploring Middle-earth. Dad beating people up in *Grand Theft Auto*. That's kind of weird."

"It's a kind of weird that I'm okay with," Mom said. "And you know what? You're a kind of weird I'm okay with. It occurs to me that maybe you're not so different from me after all. We're manipulative, sneaky bitches who like to snoop."

"How do you know you can trust Denise?" I asked.

"I don't," she said. "But how much less would I trust her if

I hadn't snooped at all? So, I get it. I get this newspaper thing. You want to snoop so you can know what's dangerous in the world. I'm all for it. I'm proud of you. Behind you one hundred percent."

"What about the family's good name?" I asked. "I thought I was embarrassing us all."

"You have and you do," she said. "But hey, you're committed now. I mean the damage is done. Now we move to a different phase. Now it's about fighting the good fight. So what's the next move?"

I shrugged. "There's not a next move, as far as I can tell."

"There's always a next move," Mom said. "Isn't there some other way into the execution?"

"There are only so many seats," I said. "One for the AP, three randomly selected seats, and one for the local paper, which isn't me."

"And two of those random seats are set aside for television reporters, but one is for a randomly selected newspaper, right? Newspaper reporters show up and draw straws or whatever?"

"Yeah, but what's the chance I'll get that?" I said. "I mean, there will probably be five or six news outlets trying to get in, and even if I get it, they could tell me I'm not a real newspaper and turn me away."

"You've come this far," Mom said. "Heck, I'll drive you out there myself if I have to."

"You really want me to try it?" I asked.

"I'd be disappointed if you didn't," Mom said.

"At first I was relieved," I told Blanderson later. "It was good to know that Dad isn't cheating. And then I thought about the whole situation. And I don't feel better at all."

I didn't intend to share my whole life story with a teacher. But there we were, already scheduled for some after-school newspaper time, and we found ourselves without as much work as we expected. So I spent the whole ninety minutes spilling everything about my home life to Blanderson. Cakes, clowns, Legos, landline phones, and all.

"I can't believe I'm telling you this," I said. "Giving all my secrets to a teacher. I mean, that's only something you do if you're abused or neglected or whatever, right? I'm breaking the rules."

"It's just two people talking," she said. "There don't have to be rules."

"Admit it," I said. "You guys live for these moments, right? The student who finally opens up and tells you everything. You could write a paper about it for some educational research journal. You'd have to change my name to protect my identity. Can I pick the name?"

Blanderson shook her head, but with a knowing smile that said, Yes, teachers do live for this stuff. Then she looked me in the eye and put both of her hands flat on her desk.

"Do me a favor," she said. "If we're going to talk seriously about your problems, stop being Smart Lisa for once. This is the problem with smart people. They say something, then they realize how it sounds, and they say something about what they just said, and then they heap on another layer of meaning and another. Stop thinking about thinking, and just talk to me. If you had to tell me in a quick sentence, tell me what's bothering you."

"Okay," I said. "It's bothering me that my dad's not having an affair."

Blanderson blinked in surprise. So I went on.

"Just think about it," I said. "Mom's really hard on him. They fight all the time. I feel like she starts it much of the time. And I always felt like that was okay because, you know, he's a cheater. But if he's not a cheater, then she's just a . . . I don't know. All the words I can think of here, I can't say, because you'll say they're antifeminist. Even the spying made sense when I thought he was a cheater. I mean, I wanted to spy too. But now it seems creepy and controlling."

"I can't believe I'm saying this," Blanderson said, "but if it's any consolation, your dad could totally still be a cheater. I mean, he could be sleeping with Denise or any other number of women."

"You're just trying to make me feel better," I said. We both laughed.

"Let's look at it like a news story," Blanderson said. "I think the real reason you were reluctant to discuss this with your dad or your mom was that you didn't have enough to publish, as it were. There was no real evidence he was cheating, just your suspicion. I don't know if you can ever prove that he's *not* cheating. If you find some jewelry and a note addressed to Denise, then I'd say he's cheating. But you didn't find that. And if you find, I don't know, a bill for pay-per-view movies that shows he rented *Transformers* films in his hotel room every day for a week, I guess it supports the theory that he's not cheating, but it doesn't prove it. Some things you just can't get to the bottom of. Trust has to come into the relationship at some point."

"Well, it doesn't sound like trust has come into the relationship for Mom," I said. "Why is she always so intense?"

Blanderson shrugged.

"Look, I don't know your mom," she said. "But I know that when people have trust issues, there's usually history behind it.

You mentioned that they used to fight a lot more than they do now. Maybe your dad committed some kind of indiscretion early in the relationship, maybe even before you were born. Something that set all this off. Did your mom mention anything like that?"

"No," I said. "And I didn't ask. I should go back and ask."

Blanderson leaned back.

"You know, maybe you should ask yourself how deep you want to get into the evil at the heart of man," she said. "There's a tendency, when you're digging, to think you haven't found the real truth until you've found something ugly. Something new to pout about. But what if that thing doesn't exist? How long do you dig and dig expecting to find it? When do you stop?"

"When I understand why they fight all the time," I said. "I mean, it's literally all they do."

"Look, couples fight," Blanderson said. "I had to find this out the hard way. My parents never fought in front of us. When things got bad between them, they'd pack me and my brother off to Grandma's house. I knew something was strange. My grandma lived just down the road, but every couple of weeks or so Grandma would get this burning desire to have us spend the night. I had my first really serious relationship in college—in fact, he'd already asked me to marry him, and I'd told him we should wait a while, and he was okay with that. And then one day we had a raging argument that started with a disagreement about the dumbest thing. Toppings on a pizza, of all things. And I left him for good. It was our first real fight, but I'd never seen couples fighting, so I thought something was really wrong with the relationship. Months later I tell the story to my mom, and she tells me the whole story of Grandma's house."

"I don't know if I want to have a relationship if it's just fighting all the time," I said.

"What relationship do you have that isn't fighting all the time?" Blanderson said. "We're fighting right now. Does that make me not your teacher, and does it make you not my student?"

I chuckled.

"But we're not fighting," I said. "Just because I raised my voice a little, and you raised your voice, and you accused me of pouting and all that, that doesn't . . . I mean, I realize that to somebody who just walked by, it would look like a fight, but we're actually having a conversation."

Blanderson just held out her hands as if to say: See?

"I bet you don't pick on Coach Sanderson the way Mom picks on Dad," I said.

"I'm starting to see the value of being more forceful," Blanderson said. "With Coach Sanderson, everything I say is just a suggestion unless I frame it as an explicit order. It's like training a dog or programming a robot. I've caught him literally taking allergy medication prescribed to our dog. He couldn't believe I got onto him about it. The vet said it was the same as the Zyrtec they give to humans but in a smaller dose, so he just did the math and took two and a half pills."

"Did the doctor explicitly say humans shouldn't take it?" I asked.

Blanderson slapped her hand on the desk.

"You shouldn't have to be told not to take a dog's medicine!" she said.

Witness

Three days before Alabama executes an inmate, a lawyer comes to the governor's office and puts a file on her desk. A summary of the case. She reviews the file and decides whether to go forward with the execution.

She could say no, switching the death sentence to life in prison. It's the only clemency power she has. If you rob a bank or smoke a joint and you want a pardon, you go to the parole board. The governor decides whether you live or die.

Seven execution files landed on the last governor's desk. In total, they added up to fifty-seven pages of material. That's according to Lew East, who did a public records request for them all.

The governor spent about an hour going over Houser's case. Again, that's according to Lew's reporting. That means the decision was made around 2:00 p.m. on Friday, around the time the bell rang for Blanderson's class.

"So you're going anyway," Blanderson said.

"I am," I said.

"Your mom is taking you?"

"No, my dad," I said. "He's back from Vegas already. Thanks to Houser's lawyers and the stay of execution. Lew East told me I should have expected a delay while the courts looked at his case again. Apparently that happens all the time."

"So it could be delayed again," Blanderson said.

"It could not happen at all," I said.

The rest of life, however, went on. At 2:40 p.m. I lined up at the front of the school with the fifteen-and-under crowd. At this point, I was probably the oldest kid in the pickup line. Ninth-grade sweethearts held hands in front of me, looking over their shoulder to make sure the teachers didn't see. To my right were a couple of besties clutching piccolo cases to their chests, each on the phone trying to convince her parents to let them have a sleepover. And there was me standing alone, refreshing a Google News search for "death warrant" on my phone.

Two days before the execution, guards move the prisoner from his normal cell to a "deathwatch" cell, right next to the execution chamber. He's been living for years in an eight-by-twelve cell that he has all to himself, where he spends twenty-three hours a day surrounded by the stuff the prison will let him have: books, magazines, maybe a television. Now he moves to a cell with just a bed, a toilet, and a table, where he's watched closely to make sure he doesn't commit suicide. If it happened on the usual schedule—again, according to Lew East—Houser would have moved to deathwatch at about 8:00 a.m. on Saturday.

I was just out of bed at the time, staring into the refrigerator and thinking about what to eat for breakfast. The kitchen phone—the Denise phone—rang. I didn't answer.

A few hours after an inmate moves to deathwatch, medics

who work in the prison system go over the inmate's medical file. They may come into the deathwatch cell and do a physical exam. Their job is to determine if the inmate is sufficiently healthy to be executed. Lew has never been able to find out what "sufficiently healthy" means, but he suspects they're just looking for a vein that's easy to stick a needle in.

Back in Beachside at the time when this would have happened for Houser, I was in the car with my parents, heading to see the latest Pixar movie. I had no desire to see the thing, but Mom and Dad are all about doing little kid stuff with me. It's one of maybe three things on the planet they agree on.

"We're not going to have you with us much longer," Mom likes to say. "You're growing up too fast."

On the day before the execution, the inmate receives visitors. Family members and friends, if the inmate has any, can come to the deathwatch cell and sit with the inmate and talk, under the watch of a guard. Jailhouse ministers almost always stop in and sometimes spend hours with the inmate. It's not clear who, if anyone, met with Matthew John Houser on the day before his execution.

"They'll release a statement that has all those details in it, just before or just after the execution," said Lew East, sounding tinny on speakerphone as Dad and I chopped up vegetables for ratatouille. We always wind up making ratatouille after seeing a Pixar movie, something we've done since I was a little kid.

The ratatouille came out well, soft like rags, with just enough onion and garlic. Matthew John Houser ate alone in his cell that day. Neither Lew nor I could find a prison menu for that weekend, though I did find a photo someone posted online of a "typical" Holman Prison meal. Yellow plastic tray, a pool of pulled-pork-like meat with a bun, a scoop of mashed potatoes that would fit nicely on an ice-cream cone, steamed carrots, and a tiny brownie.

At dinnertime, the guards would also have brought him a menu so he could choose his last meal for the next day. The rule is, the prisoner who's going to be executed can eat anything that's on the prison menu, so he would have basically picked his prison-food favorites.

On the morning of an execution, guards take the inmate out of his cell and move him to the prison's showers, where he showers under the watch of a guard. Then he's issued "appropriate clothing" for the execution and sent back to his cell. That's what state officials told Lew, anyway.

It's not clear why the Department of Corrections has a checklist item just for this shower, but it suggests inmates don't bathe every day. Lew thinks "appropriate clothing" means prison scrubs that actually fit. Lew says that in prisons and jails, inmates' clothes get washed together, and you're lucky to get back all the clothes that are issued to you. Even your underwear might have been worn by somebody else.

In Beachside, the morning of the execution was fresh and cold, with fog rising from the river and the hills.

We left for the prison at about 7:00 a.m., the time I normally would have been getting to school, but for some reason it seemed earlier in the morning, like we were fishermen setting off just before sunrise, our car the only moving thing in the landscape.

"Are you sure that's what you want to wear?" Mom said as she leaned in through the car window to kiss me good-bye.

"Lew said formal but not too formal, like a stranger's funeral," I said. "Black seems appropriate."

"Yes, but in this light you can see that the turtleneck is a darker black than the skirt," Mom said. "The textures don't really go together."

"Nobody's going to really be looking at her," Dad said. "You know how reporters dress. Tan pants and a blue Oxford shirt. Boring. Cheap. Nondescript."

Mom shook her head. "Well, Lisa, you've found the perfect job for your fashion sense."

Ah, Mom. Over the next five hours, we drove through tiny towns, down mountainsides that made our ears pop, through Birmingham and past its skyscrapers—Dad never takes bypasses, convinced that a straight line has to be faster—and south to places that were flatter and warmer. Lots to see and lots to think about, but thanks to Mom I must have looked down to compare my skirt and my turtleneck a thousand times.

"It's interstate almost all the way," Dad said. "Easy peasy. Don't you want to drive a little? You did finally take the learner's permit test, didn't you?"

I shook my head. "When have I *ever* wanted to drive?"

An inmate's last meal probably happens about three hours before the execution, around 2:30 p.m. Of the last ten men executed before Houser, eight wanted a hamburger. Five also wanted fried chicken. Mashed potatoes was a side item in seven of those final meals.

From Montgomery to Atmore, our drive was a grind of boredom. The land was flat, the towns tiny. Then in the distance, we saw a single tall building off the interstate.

"That would be the hotel at the Creek casino," Dad said. "So we're almost there. Look, we can stop in Atmore for something to eat before we go to the prison. You'll be in there for a while."

All I could think about was last meals. What's it like to finish a cup of mashed potatoes knowing you'll never eat anything again? That soon you won't even be able to think about eating?

"I'm a little hungry," I said. "But I just don't think I can eat right now."

"You okay?" he said.

"Yeah," I said. "I'm okay."

We never did get close to the casino and the hotel on that drive. Siri had us take an exit that seemed to lead nowhere. A two-lane road through flat country where brown, harvested fields lined both sides of the road. Signs said the prison was close. But you really had to look to see it. Just a gray line of fence in the distance.

"I don't get it," I said as we approached a gate. "Where's the actual prison?"

"In there somewhere, I guess," Dad said. "I suppose if anyone escapes, they want them to have a long run."

The guard immediately guessed what we were there for.

"Execution?" he said. "Name?"

He checked us against a list.

"You're not family of the inmate or the victim," he said.

"Media," Dad said.

"Not here," the guard said.

"Not me," Dad said. "Her."

The guard went into his shack and was on the phone for several minutes. When he came out, he looked ticked off but didn't say why. He just handed Dad a piece of paper.

"Put this in your window. Turn right at the turn. Go to Building 2120," he said.

We moved on, passing vast empty fields and little clusters of white buildings. Building 2120 was just another one of those buildings, a windowless cinder-block number with a TV truck and a few other cars parked outside. A single door was propped open with a folding chair.

"I guess this is it," Dad said. "Are you sure you're okay? Want me to go in with you?"

I took a deep breath. I hate meeting bunches of new people, even under the best conditions.

"No, I think having a parent around would just underscore the fact that I'm a kid," I said. I grabbed a notepad and a pen. "Just wait here and I'll tell you what to do."

Before I even got to the door, a tall, kind of disturbingly handsome man in a suit emerged. The name on his nametag surprised me. I don't know why I'd never bothered to look up a photo of Tyburn Riggs. Why was I surprised that he was young and Black and he wore tailored clothes?

"You must be Ms. Woodley-Rives," he said. He extended a hand, but his tone was severe, as if he were processing an inmate.

"So, Tyburn Riggs," I said. "You're a lot younger than I thought you'd be."

He nodded. "What an interesting thing to say," he said. "I want to make clear, again, that there's no guarantee at all that you'll be able to witness the execution. When we hold the lottery for the open seat, if you don't get the seat, you'll be required to stay here until all the events are concluded. That could mean you'll be here late into the night, if the court delays the execution."

"Understood," I said.

"So you do want to be on the list for the randomly selected seat?" he asked.

"Yes," I said. "You say 'randomly selected.' What does that mean? How do you do the selection?"

"We don't release that information," Riggs said. "Look, here's a packet with some basic information you'll need. If you go into the prison for the execution, you'll have to consent to a search, and you'll bring in only the notepads and pencils we provide. But we've waived our rules on cell phones and laptops in this area, so you can write and post from here."

I grabbed the laptop from the car and sent Dad on his way. Inside the white building, there was one long room lined with wood paneling and filled with folding banquet tables. A podium, with no one behind it, stood at the far end of the room. There were already TV cameras set up around it. At one of the banquet tables sat a handful of worried-looking people staring at computer screens. One of them, a short, pudgy white guy with a broad grin, jumped up and waved.

"Lisa! You're Lisa," he said. "Lew East. Welcome to prison."

As I settled in, Matthew John Houser ate his last meal—taco salad, turnip greens with ham, chocolate cake for dessert. That's according to an announcement in one of the sheets of paper Riggs gave me, with a heading on top that said, EMBARGOED UNTIL AFTER EXECUTION IS CARRIED OUT. Also in the announcement: Houser got special permission to watch a *Lord of the Rings* movie, on a prison staffer's laptop, while he ate.

"I need more information," said Judy Gilliam, the Associated Press reporter. I'd read her stories a hundred times, and now I was sitting right next to her. No makeup, hair tied back, in a pantsuit that made me feel better because I was pretty sure the coat and pants weren't the same shade of black. She carried her laptop and notepads in what was clearly a repurposed diaper bag.

"Aren't there three *Lord of the Rings* movies?" she said. "Which one did he watch?"

"And how much will he get to see?" Lew asked. "I mean, I hate to be crude, but we've got three hours to go. They'll be moving him to the death chamber in a couple of hours."

I stared at my computer and typed like everyone else. Judy and Lew and the reporter from *Birmingham Buzz* and TV people farther down the table eating fast food and editing video on their laptops and talking to one another without looking up. It's good that they weren't looking up. Because I suddenly felt a little light-headed.

"Okay over there, Lisa?" Lew asked. "These details can be really ghoulish, I realize. I guess I should be more creeped out than I am. But you'll find in the end that these are the things that make readers care."

Judy nodded. "Never underestimate the narrative power of the last meal," she said. Then she turned to me and smiled. "But, you know, I should have realized that since it's your first time here, you might have some questions. Anything?"

"Umm," I said. "I don't want to look like a dummy, but this doesn't feel right. We're just *waiting* here. Am I supposed to be asking Riggs some questions?"

"This is my favorite part of prison," Lew said. "They take away most of your stuff and make you wait. And wait. A pleasant break from deadlines."

Judy shook her head. "Prewriting is your friend," she said. "Whenever I have downtime like this, I'm writing the story that I'll publish afterward. See, I've got all this background material, and I've left a space here for last words and all that. So I can post as soon as possible. You're going to post a story tonight, right?"

"Yes." I guess I should be posting my story tonight, I thought. I took out my phone and started texting Blanderson.

"Other than that," Lew said, "we just wait."

I opened a new window on my laptop and found a pirated *Fellowship of the Ring* on YouTube. It ran with the subtitles on as I started writing what I could already say about the execution.

As I typed, the Dark Lord, Sauron, created the One Ring. Things that should never be forgotten were lost. Bilbo Baggins vanished and Frodo and Sam set out across the Shire with the Ring. In a golden field, Sam stopped in his tracks. One more step, he said, and he'd be farther from home than he'd ever traveled in his life.

About thirty minutes before the execution, doctors give the inmate a cup of water and a couple of sedative pills, just to steady his nerves. I don't know if the inmate is required to take them. According to Lew, no one ever refuses.

Tyburn Riggs entered the room and went to the podium. We all gathered our notepads and rushed toward him. Bright camera lights came on.

"This is nothing you'll want to film, unless you need B-roll," he said. Then, reading from a piece of paper, he said, "The execution is moving forward, and we're about to begin the process of moving the witnesses to the execution chamber. You will be entering Holman Prison. Television cameramen will be allowed to board the bus to film outside the prison but will not enter the chamber. You will be allowed to bring only a single pad of paper and a pencil, both of which we provide for you. No other objects will be allowed. Those of you who witness the execution will be pool reporters, and by going in you consent to do on-camera interviews and to otherwise be a source for other reporters on what happened in the execution chamber. If you do not consent to this, you shouldn't go into the chamber."

I looked around at the faces in the crowd. Everybody looked as nervous as me.

"Here's who will be entering the chamber," Riggs continued and read off the list of names. Then he said, "And finally, Lew East from the Minden paper will enter the chamber as our randomly selected witness from a print outlet."

I knew I should have spoken up again with my question about how the random selection is done. But Lew jumped in first.

"How many papers actually sought the random seat?" he asked.

"I believe only two," Riggs said. "Minden and the student publication known as the *Beachside Bulletin*."

"Can you verify that?" Lew said. "Just two? Are you sure?"

"If you consider the *Bulletin* a newspaper, then two," Riggs said.

"Then I withdraw our entry in the lottery," Lew said. Everyone turned to look at Lew. "Yes, I know my editors will be ticked. I mean, they sent me all the way down here. But I'm withdrawing."

"You can do that," Riggs said. "But then there won't be a random seat in the pool."

"That's not how it works, Tyburn, and you know it," Lew said. "Twice I've witnessed executions because another outlet backed out of the random slot. Remember the woman from the Tuscaloosa paper who had the panic attack and couldn't go in? And you gave it to me instead."

Riggs shook his head. "We're really very short on time," he said. "I can check, but if I don't get word very shortly, it's you or no one."

A faint buzz. Riggs picked a cell phone up off the podium, looked at it.

"Very well," he said. "I just got word from the commissioner of the Department of Corrections. If Minden withdraws, the representative from the *Beachside Bulletin* goes in."

"That was quick," said a camera guy. "Is somebody live streaming all this?"

The little press conference broke up. Riggs said we had five minutes to use the bathroom and then line up for a search. Lew walked up to me.

"Nobody's live streaming," he said. "The commissioner was standing over there, in the back of the room, the whole time. Don't know where he's gone to now."

"Well, I guess I ought to thank him," I said. "And you. If 'thank' is the right word."

"Maybe it isn't," Lew said. "Maybe you'll regret doing this. Most people who are involved in an execution, in any way, have some kind of regret. You won't feel it today or tomorrow maybe, but it will come."

"Now you're making me nervous," I said.

"You're going to be nervous," he said. "You're going to be scared and maybe disgusted. When it happens, just think to yourself that what you're feeling is natural. And keep writing. Keep paying attention to the details. It's your job."

We all loaded quietly onto a short bus. Witnesses and guys with bulky cameras and tripods, who were going only part of the way, to get video of the outside of the prison. After everyone had boarded, Tyburn Riggs went up to the front and whispered something to the driver.

The bus trundled out of the parking lot onto a winding road

through the fenced-in expanse, then out onto the highway and past another guard shack and fence on the other side of the highway. Another winding road. The prison grounds were huge, flat, featureless. I tried to make sense of the landscape as I looked out the window, but all I could see were one-story white cinder-block buildings and fences. No signs, not along the road or on the buildings.

We pulled to a stop at the bottom of a small hill. Atop the hill stood a cluster of larger white buildings surrounded by a tall fence with another fence around it. At each corner of the fence, there was a tower. We'd already passed one fence and then another, but this was the real prison, the place where the inmates slept and ate and lived out their lives.

"This is a place where you can shoot some B-roll," Riggs said in a soft voice. "We'll stay here for five minutes or so before proceeding into the facility. This is B-roll only. No live stand-ups, please."

B-roll is the video they run in the background, on television, while the anchors are talking. Shots of planes landing and taking off, for instance, if they're talking about an airport.

I didn't have a camera, but the other print reporters stood and got off the bus, so I did too. Look closely at the towers, and you could see guards with rifles. The buildings had few windows. The grass was cut so short it almost seemed like tan paint on bare rock.

A gusty wind buffeted us as the TV crew and *Birmingham Buzz* set up cameras in the middle of the road. We stood there, right on the stripe in the road. No one was coming. Far as the eye could see, roads and buildings. The prison complex was like a ghost city.

Then I heard voices. From the nearest building, where there

were a few long slits that must have served as windows. Men's voices, screaming against the wind.

"Help us!" one voice said. "It's inhumane in here! This is unconstitutional!" It was hard to make out an individual voice in the jumble, but they were all saying stuff like that. I wrote down what I could.

"Those guys know how to play the press," Riggs said softly, either to me or to a nearby camerawoman. "This wing closest to us, this is the newest death-row wing. About a hundred of our condemned inmates are in there. No matter what they say, they have cells to themselves and good food and even television. I'd feel just fine if none of their complaints wound up on the news."

I said nothing. The camerawoman shrugged. "I can't get the sound with this wind anyway," she said.

Quiet. Wind. Distant screams.

"Are we good?" Riggs said, his voice still subdued. "All right, let's go."

We rode in silence through a gate, and then another, and then another. We parked amid a jumble of small buildings. Just a minute earlier there had been plenty of light, with the sun near setting. Now, with the sun blocked by the surrounding buildings, it suddenly seemed much darker, much later in the day. We got out of the bus and waited, standing in the bus headlights, as guards counted our heads and counted again. More screams, louder, about bad food and innocence and racism. Somehow I had thought inmates would be yelling sexual stuff, harassing us. But there was just this.

Riggs motioned us to enter a building that looked like a portable classroom. We went single file down a narrow hallway and then into a small room where twelve folding chairs sat facing a window covered by a reddish curtain on the other side. The first two rows of chairs were already filled, and the people sitting looked like they were waiting for a puppet show to begin. Riggs pointed, showing us we should fill in the last row.

This is it, I realized. This is the place. Suddenly I felt a claustrophobic kind of panic. It wasn't the size of the room, though that was part of it. It was me, there, a high school sophomore in that place with all those adults around me. As I sat, I had a sudden sick feeling like I was being strapped into a roller coaster. I was stuck there until the ride was over.

"Everyone, please," Riggs said, "we ask that you say nothing until the execution is complete. If for some reason you have an emergency and feel you have to leave, just knock lightly on the door." And he left us.

Silence among strangers. Panic inside me. I hoped it didn't show. Not because I was embarrassed, but because it seemed wrong, morally wrong, to have emotions there. I took Lew's advice. *Keep on writing.*

In the front row were two young women in black pantsuits. Houser's lawyers, I guessed, but I didn't write that down, because I didn't know for sure. They whispered to each other occasionally. One white and dirty blonde, the other with a tan complexion and jet-black hair. The lawyer I'd spoken with on the phone? She didn't look like her publicity photo. More heavyset, puffy eyed, an expression of resignation on her face.

In the second row, three middle-aged white women with short hair, one with reading glasses dangling from her neck. Each sat with hands folded, though one occasionally wiped away tears. I wasn't sure who they were. Houser had no family that claimed him, as far as I knew. Also in that row, to my right, a gray-haired white man, skinny like a runner, in slacks and a yellow button-up shirt. I could see that there was a Bible on his lap.

We sat for a long time. I could hear the breath of every person in the room. So clearly that I could tell when people were crying a few seconds before they wiped their eyes. I listened to my own breathing. This thing that was all of life. On the other side of that curtain, Houser was breathing too, and thinking that each breath was one of only a few left to him.

I didn't want the curtain to open.

I closed my eyes and tried to make my breath calm.

I heard the curtain opening.

Houser was close, uncomfortably close to us. He was already strapped to the table, which seemed to sit just a couple of feet from the window. The room he was in was small. Houser didn't look like the punk kid in the yearbook photos. He looked like a war veteran. Head shaved bald. Super lean, like a marathon runner. In orange-brown jumpsuit-like scrubs, making him look a little like someone who'd just gotten off work at a hospital. His left arm, the one I could see, was sinewy, veiny. There was a white band on it with tubes coming out. Those tubes ran to somewhere I couldn't see, some place where the poisons that would kill him would be administered. Two men in suits stood near him. One was talking on a landline phone on the wall. The other stood quietly facing away from us with a big leather Bible in his right hand. That's all I could see of him: back, arm, hand, Bible.

On the other side of the execution chamber, there was another window. To the room where the victim's family was allowed to view the execution. The window wasn't far from us, really, but it was darkened, so I couldn't see inside or tell if anyone was there. Houser turned to look into that window. I think his mouth moved. Then he turned to look at us. To look at me, just for a second. That's why I say he looked like a vet-eran—there was an intense look in his eyes. Fear, I guess. But the fear of a guy who's about to jump off a diving board. The intensity of a guy who's trying to convince himself he's ready.

His eyes scanned the room and softened when they settled on the women I thought were lawyers. He managed a nervous smile. I think he mouthed the words "Thank you."

The man on the phone hung up. A speaker crackled to life. "I've just spoken to the governor. The governor has given the order, and the execution of Matthew John Houser will commence at 5:30 p.m. Mr. Houser will first be given the opportunity to make a final statement." The man stood to the side of the chamber, his back to us.

Houser looked at the other window. Then at us. Then up at the ceiling.

"There was no treasure," he said. "There is no treasure. If I had known that, I wouldn't have done what I did. I'm sorry to everybody. I love you all, and I wish I had done better."

Another crackle as the speaker went off. Only after I heard scribbling next to me did I think to write down his last statement.

Then the waiting. Houser looked up at the ceiling. His face was a mask, blank. His fist clenched, the muscles in his arm roiling. Fear. His mouth moved. He said something but the microphone was off. He wasn't looking at the man with the Bible, but he was clearly having a conversation with him. The man with the Bible grabbed Houser's hand and knelt by the table where Houser lay. The man's lips moved. Praying. Houser watched, his eyes glassy. The man with the Bible stood and Houser leaned back again. He seemed more relaxed, whether because of the drugs or because of the prayer.

For a long while, the only thing that moved was Houser's

chest. Big, slow breaths. He was looking up at the ceiling again, his eyes growing glassier. I could only imagine what lying there waiting to die must feel like. Like falling through your bed in a nightmare? Everything falling away. Knowing you'll never eat macaroni again or watch TV or hold a baby. Falling back into a tunnel where no one can follow you, where you'll lie alone forever. I realized my own panicked breathing was becoming audible. Back to note-taking. Just the facts.

The women in the front row, who might have been big-time lawyers from New York, were openly weeping. The short-haired woman who'd wiped away tears before was crying and softly blew her nose. The other two women were calm and quiet, looking at no one but Houser. The man in the second row with the Bible in his lap opened it. To the book of Philippians. I strained to make out the chapter and verse, squinting because I didn't want to lean forward, didn't want to move at all.

Houser changed in some way, as if a wave had washed over him. His face became slack, relaxed. His eyes seemed to slowly close, though it was hard to tell for sure. There was a wet gleam there for a while and then there wasn't. The muscular arm seemed to go slack. His bald head, his face, became a darker pink.

That's the end, I thought. But then the chest moved, a short sharp catch.

We sat for more long minutes. Philippians Man finished reading, closed his Bible, looked up toward the ceiling, then bowed his head. Another catch in Houser's chest. A long while later, another.

And then some other wave seemed to pass through Houser. I can't explain it. His skin turned from pink to almost orange. His mouth fell open. He seemed to settle, to get smaller. I felt like I was seeing a man crumble slowly into an orange skeleton.

He seemed so skinny, as if he were not the same person we'd been watching just minutes before.

Then something else seemed to change; I don't know what. The two lawyers began to whisper frantically to each other. The man standing near the phone turned quickly and closed the curtain.

The door opened and Tyburn Riggs entered. "The execution of Matthew John Houser is complete," he said. "We'll exit the room in an orderly fashion, with our media representatives in the back row exiting first."

Out to the courtyard, where it was pitch black except for the bus headlights. If there was still screaming, I didn't hear it. Onto the bus. Nobody spoke. Nobody wanted to. Backing out with a beep, then through the gates, then onto the empty prison road.

"Okay," said Judy from AP. "I have 'There was no treasure. There is no treasure. If I had known that, I wouldn't have done it. I'm sorry to everybody. I love you all, and I wish I had done better.' Does that match what everybody else has?"

"I have 'wouldn't have done what I did,'" said a guy from one of the TV stations.

"Me too," said the reporter from *Birmingham Buzz*. "What I did."

Judy nodded and wrote in her notebook. "I'm okay with 'what I did,' as long as we all agree," she said. She turned to look at me. "Lisa?"

I guess I was in shock. First I nodded. Then I looked at my notes. "Yes," I said, nodding too emphatically. "'What I did.' That's what I've got."

I felt nothing. A huge foggy amount of nothing. I had done nothing. We had done nothing. We had sat and watched a man die. It wasn't like we had gone into combat.

But I guess something about us seemed different. As we filed back into the paneled room, all the other media folks stood and watched us. With worried, respectful looks, like we'd just survived a horrible disaster. Even Lew looked at me differently.

The cameras were on. When a TV camera's on you, it's hot. The lights—you can feel them even with your eyes closed.

Nobody said a word. Riggs headed to the back of the room, to the podium. We all followed him. The two groups—the journalists who'd gone in and the ones who'd stayed back—merged into a gaggle of reporters.

"Is everybody ready?" Riggs said at the podium. "We're only going to do this once, and it's going to be brief. Everyone?"

He paused for a minute, looking down at his notes, looking like a man in prayer. Then he said, "The execution of Matthew John Houser was carried out at 5:30 p.m. central standard time in the execution chamber at Holman Prison. Mr. Houser was found guilty of the capital murders of Elbert and Jennifer Williams in Beachside. Mr. Houser was declared dead at 5:55 p.m. central standard time. No one has claimed his body, and he will be buried in Holman's prison cemetery if his body is not claimed.

"Witnesses to his execution include members of the media, two representatives from his legal team, two volunteers from the group Against the Death Penalty, and two Methodist ministers. Mr. Houser was counseled in the chamber by his own minister. Mr. Houser had no immediate family, and none of his more distant relatives chose to witness the execution. Mr. Houser's family has issued no statement. There were no witnesses from the victims' family. They've asked that you respect their privacy, and they haven't issued a statement. You have information about Mr. Houser's last meal in your packet. In the hours before his death, Mr. Houser watched a film, a special request that the warden consented to, and met with the ministers who later witnessed the execution. He had no other visitors. The media witnesses to the execution are acting as pool reporters and have agreed to act as sources for the rest of you. I'll ask them now to come to the podium and answer your questions about the execution and how it was carried out."

In the knot of reporters, we turned to look at one another. Worry on every face. Reporters aren't supposed to be the story, yet there we were. I looked to Judy, the obvious leader of our group, but she was calmly tweeting an update, as if she hadn't heard Riggs's call for witnesses.

And then a strange thing happened. I moved out of the crowd and toward the podium. It was almost as if I were watching somebody else do it. I still don't know why I started walking, but no one followed me. I was alone at the podium. The camera lights were hot, and I couldn't really see anyone's face.

"All right," I said. "I'm Lisa Rives of the *Beachside Bulletin*. R-I-V-E-S, rhymes with 'leaves.'"

"What's your position with the *Bulletin*?" asked a voice from the light.

"Editor. Editor in chief," I said.

"Lisa," said Lew's voice. "Tell us what you saw. Just the facts."

"The facts," I said. "We entered the room. Sat and waited. The curtain opened. Houser was already strapped to the table when the curtain opened. A member of the prison staff announced that the execution would proceed. They gave him a chance to say his last words."

I stopped. I didn't have my notes in front of me.

"I have it here," came Judy's voice. "'There was no treasure. There is no treasure.' Folks, I have the complete statement here, and I'll email it to each of you."

"Lisa," said another voice from the light. "Do you have any idea what he meant by this 'treasure' thing?"

I had my questions about it. I wanted to discuss them. But I kept what Lew had said in mind. Just the facts.

"I really couldn't speculate," I said.

"What happened after the statement?" Lew asked.

I took a deep breath.

"Houser looked up to the ceiling," I said. "His mouth moved, but the microphone was off. A man with a Bible, who was in the room with Houser and who may have been a chaplain, knelt and held Houser's hand. The chaplain's lips moved. I would guess that he was praying. Then the chaplain stood, and over the next, well, many minutes, Houser continued to look at the ceiling. Then his eyes closed. His muscles seemed to relax. After a time, his chest stopped moving. Sometime later, Mr. Riggs said he was dead."

"That's all?" asked a voice from the light. "We have tweets from his lawyers who were in the chamber with you. They say his left eye popped open during the execution—a sign that the drugs may not have put him under. Did you see that?"

"I didn't," I said.

There was a rumble in the crowd. I had a sinking feeling. If his eye did open, that was a big story. A botched execution. Did that happen, and I just missed it?

"Lisa," said Lew. "Tell us what you did see. Right at the end of the process."

"Houser's lawyers were sitting in front of us," I said. "I saw one of them turn to the other in what seemed to be surprise or alarm. Then the prison staffer moved to shut the drape, and Mr. Riggs came in and declared the execution was over."

"From where you were," said another voice, "could you have seen his eyes open?"

"Maybe," I said. "I understand why they would have said only the left eye. It was the only one visible to us, where we were sitting. I wasn't focusing on his eyes at the time. I was looking at his chest, his arm, for signs of movement and, well, color change."

"I'd concur with what Lisa says," said Judy. "I couldn't rule out an eye opening. But I didn't see it."

"Me either," someone else said.

"What does it feel like, to watch someone die?" said a voice. I could see some heads turning, in surprise, at that question. Shocked looks, the kind I get so often at school.

"I can't really say what it feels like," I said. "I don't think my feelings are relevant here. But I really have to think about it. To process it. I'm just here to get the facts. Any factual questions?"

A few seconds of silence. Then Lew spoke, in a surprisingly soft voice.

"Lisa," he said. "How old are you?"

"I'm fifteen," I said.

Dad wanted to hug me.

"Not here," I said. "Let's go."

Reporters were packing up, their stories complete and on the web. The camera lights were swinging across the parking lot.

"You've already sent your story in?" Dad said. "Okay, I'll put the laptop in the trunk and we'll go."

We backed out of the parking lot, worked our way through the prison roads and out through the gates. Not a word from either of us until we were on the real highway in the real world.

"No radio?" I asked.

"I thought you might want a break," Dad said.

"That's probably a good idea," I said.

"I'll put on some classical if you like," Dad said. "I saw you on TV. Impressive. Good work. Do you want to talk about it? Anything you want to get off your chest?"

I searched my feelings. Still a fog of nothing.

"I think for the first time in my life, I don't want to talk about it," I said. "I don't have anything to say."

"Fair enough," Dad said. "The door's open anytime if you want to talk."

"I'm tired," I said. "I feel old and tired."

Dad shrugged.

"Take a nap," he said. "It's not that far from bedtime. It'll help you process. And your loud snoring will keep me awake."

He never did put on classical music. I leaned the seat back a bit and watched the Creek casino pass. Then we were out on the interstate, with its billboards advertising great places to eat and rest and take a shower. I had nothing to say about them. No condescension for truck stop food, no pity for people who shower at gas stations. Eating and showering are things you do when you are alive. It was hard to think of anything beyond that.

At some point I did fall asleep. A fitful dream, like you have when you have the flu. I was in the paneled room. My laptop for some reason was stuck inside the restroom there. I couldn't open the door enough to get it out. And then I was awake again.

"There is no treasure," I said.

"What?" Dad said.

"That's what he said," I said. "There was no treasure. There is no treasure. And he watched *Lord of the Rings* before the execution."

"And you're wondering what it means," Dad said.

"I guess," I said. "Maybe I'm struggling with it. I mean, his imaginary world. Not orcs and wizards and all that. But the idea that there's a soundtrack, a sidekick. An adventure. A camera that follows one hero. A hero. He believed it like we all seem to believe it. But there is no treasure."

Dad just nodded.

"I think I screwed it up," I said. "Some witnesses are saying his eyes opened. That would mean a botched execution. It could have happened. And somehow I missed it. A botched execution that could end the death penalty and I missed it."

"I'd look at what people are saying about everything before I judge," Dad said.

I checked my phone, obscenely bright in the dark. I'd been asleep less than an hour. But my life had changed.

A text from Blanderson: "A fine story, well reported. It's been an honor to work with you on this. The traffic crashed our website. A couple of magazines have asked if they can run it."

From Preethy: "I cried when I saw you on TV. You are brave and ferocious. Whatever happens between us, I will always love you and will always be proud."

Jamie Scranton: "I was wrong. This is important journalistic work. You persevered in the face of a lot of critics, including me. My hat is off to you."

Nolan Ramsey: "You look hot in black." With a smiley-face emoji and a link to a TV clip of me at the podium.

Nolan, willing to risk anything to get a laugh or a lay. And, you know, I did laugh. I clicked on the clip—CNN!—but didn't watch much of it. Didn't have the sound on.

Calling up that clip brought up other suggested clips. Dozens of news websites and blogs had posted clips of me.

Outrage: Alabama lets 15-year-old watch execution

15-yo kicks ass, brings internet's rage on prison
officials in execution-witness video

Clemency UK, other groups call for censure of
Alabama officials after teen witnesses execution

I groaned. This was the worst possible outcome. I was the story. Not Houser. Not his victims. Before then, all the anti-death-penalty types had seemed to support my efforts to get into the execution chamber. Now my presence there was an outrage, the sign of a sick system. And everyone was so shocked, as if they'd never seen any of the coverage of my lawsuit.

"They probably haven't," Blanderson texted me after I messaged her about this. "Like my dad used to say: 'They're not hanging on our every word.' But this finally broke through the ice. You've made people care."

"But we're missing something," I said out loud, as if Blanderson could hear.

"What?" Dad said.

"Nothing," I said. "I hate this story. It's missing something. Something human."

"Mmm," Dad said, as he often did when he didn't know what to say. "We need gas, and I need to pee. Let's stop up here."

We pulled over at a gas station, the kind of place where they have chicken on a rotisserie and you smell like fried food when you leave. Dad started pumping gas. I headed for the ladies' room. Small as the store was, I expected a creepy little closet. Instead, there was a brightly lit restroom with two stalls and a two-sink counter in front of a mirror. A woman stood in front of one of the sinks, not really looking in the mirror. Just staring down at her purse, her hands. I almost didn't recognize her.

"Rhee Ann," I said. "I'm sorry. Is that you?"

It was. She looked up, and just for a moment I saw an exasperated, I'm-done-with-this look on her face. She looked at me in the mirror without turning, and when she recognized me, she smiled. Her greeting-at-the-door smile. I could tell it wasn't easy for her.

"Lisa Rives," she said. "Good to see you."

I took one step toward her and stopped. She hadn't turned toward me. "So you're here? You came for the execution?"

She rummaged in her purse as if looking for something. "I came," she said. "I was going to watch or thought I might. And then I thought, What's the point? So I rented a hotel room to stay the night. I watched the news. And then I couldn't sleep. So I'm going home."

I nodded. "I'm sorry. That's all I can say. I'm sorry you had to go through any of this."

"You have nothing to be sorry for," she said, rummaging faster, her voice gummy with emotion. "You know, I saw you shut down Houser's lawyers. You could have said you saw his eyes pop open, and you didn't. So, good for you."

"I couldn't have said that, really," I said. "Because I didn't see it. I really just want to be honest. To tell the truth. That's all I want."

She stopped rummaging and looked up at the mirror, right into my eyes. "I believe you," she said. "No, I'm serious. I see it in you. You're a good person. You just want to get it right."

"Thank you," I said.

She turned to me, picking up her purse.

"Well, so I suppose you'll want an interview?" she said.

"I'm just here to use the restroom," I said. "I'll respect your wishes."

"No, it's fine, really," she said. "I trust you. I trust your heart. What do you want to know?"

"I don't even have a notepad," I said.

Rummaging again. She handed me a lined pink to-do pad and a mini purple pen. I guess I looked surprised.

"Don't be a ninny," she said. "Take it. So. What do you want to know?"

I want to unknow, I thought. I want readers to see how devastating this is, how devastated you are. How devastated I am.

"It's a terrible question," I said. "It's the kind of question that makes people hate reporters. But I think the question I have to ask is: How do you feel?"

She looked up at the ceiling for a moment, thinking. Then back at me.

"I don't feel anything," she said.

I just let the silence lie there for a while.

"It's over," she said. "That's good. The world will forget him now, and it will forget me. And it will forget what little it knew about Jennifer, although it never really knew anything about Jennifer. But I won't forget Jennifer."

Now she was crying.

"I won't ever forget my sister, Jennifer," she said. And, still crying, she said: "It's late. You drive safe."

And she walked out.

I passed Dad on the way to the car. "I've got to pee too," he said. "Do you need anything from the store?"

"I've got an urgent update I need to make to the story," I said. "I've got to get the laptop."

He handed me the car keys.

"In the trunk," he said. "Don't close the keys in there this time, or we'll be stuck here."

There in the Black Belt, the roads were long and flat. I was sure the one pair of taillights I saw in the distance belonged to Rhee Ann's car. I went to our car and popped open the trunk. The laptop was in there, along with a gross bag of dirty clothes Dad had forgotten to bring in from his last trip. And a cardboard box that had tumbled over. Spilled out of that box: video game cases.

They were all there. Every game every teen boy talked about. *Red Dead Redemption. Fallout. GTA. Battlefield. Battlefront. Funkirk.* My sweet father plays *Funkirk.*

I got into the car. Fired up the laptop, turned my cell phone into a hot spot, and called Blanderson on speaker.

"Hi, Lisa," she said.

"You're still up," I said.

"Too worked up to sleep," she said. "Tomorrow's going to be a bear for both of us."

"I'm glad you're up," I said. "I've got new quotes, and I need to update the article. No, not an update. A rewrite. A new lead. A new focus."

"Wow," she said. "You must have a lot of new material. What have you got?"

"The real story," I said. "I've finally got at the real story."

ACKNOWLEDGMENTS

My first book, *Atty at Law*, didn't include an acknowledgments page, and there was a reason for that. When I write for young kids, I try to leave out the things that young kids skip. Some readers were genuinely amused that I dedicated the book to a dog, but I think this pleased my wife more than if I'd dedicated the book to her. If you knew our dog personally, you'd understand.

In the year since *Atty* hit bookstores, the need for thank-yous has piled up. First, family. I doubt my dad ever thought of himself as a writer, but every Saturday he locked himself in his study and agonized over what he'd say from the pulpit Sunday—so, yes, he was a working writer. My mother, a high school English teacher, is the best, most telegraphic writer I know, even though she's made it clear she has no intention of entering the ego hell that is the writer's life. I struggle to concisely say everything I need to say to thank my wife, Buffy. Let it suffice to say that if you hear a strong female voice that inspires you in either of these books, it's me channeling my mom or Buffy. Our son, Noah, has been my connection to kid culture for all these years, and now that he's past his eighteenth birthday, I worry that the literary nest will be empty. My brother Ragan, named after an ancestor and not after any president, was a good sport about my decision to create a fictional girl in *Atty at Law* with a similar name. At least she's not demon possessed.

This book is dedicated to Jerry Chandler, a journalism

instructor at Jacksonville State University who was a mentor to me, to Buffy, and to many of the journalists I know and respect. Here again I struggle to express all my gratitude—our gratitude—concisely. I suppose I shouldn't say simply that he's Blanderson. But that's it. He's Blanderson.

This book wouldn't exist at all without my own students, sent by the University of Alabama to the *Anniston Star*, where I was asked to coach them as daily reporters. All of them were excellent people who saw reporting as an adventure and wrote with passion. The very best of them were people who, like Lisa Rives, are perhaps a little too bold and need to be reined in from time to time. A conversation with a former student inspired this book, but every one of my students became part of Lisa in one way or another.

I got a real kick out of an online review of *Atty* that said the book lacked Southern charm. I never had any intention of depicting Alabama as anything other than what I see in front of me, charming or not, and it often isn't charming. But I'm also not going to dis Alabama when there's no need, so I have to acknowledge the astounding amount of warmth and support I got from people in my own community. I expected backlash to *Atty*, because I didn't pull a lot of punches about my home state. Instead I heard voices of support from the most amazing places: city employees, bank presidents, elected officials, librarians—and, yes, kids, who are the only people I actually expect to be reasonable and fair. If there's actual charm in the South, it's because of folks like y'all.

Finally, of course, I have to thank the folks at Seven Stories. Julia Gourary was an intern who rescued the *Atty* manuscript when it could have been missed. Lauren Hooker and Ruth Weiner are present in both of my books in ways the reader may not notice, because of their keen sense of what needs to be added or taken out. Let it suffice to say that without them, Jethro Gersham wouldn't have had his day in court.

ABOUT THE AUTHOR

Tim Lockette is a reporter, novelist, and teacher of journalists. He has written for *Teaching Tolerance*, the *Anniston Star* (Ala.), and the *Gainesville Sun* (Fla.), among other publications, and has done extensive reporting on Alabama's death penalty. He is the author of the middle-grade novel *Atty at Law*. He lives in Alabama.

ABOUT SEVEN STORIES PRESS

Seven Stories Press is an independent book publisher based in New York City. We publish works of the imagination by such writers as Nelson Algren, Russell Banks, Octavia E. Butler, Alex DiFrancesco, Ani DiFranco, Assia Djebar, Ariel Dorfman, Coco Fusco, Barry Gifford, Ernesto Che Guevara, Martha Long, Luis Negrón, Peter Plate, Hwang Sok-yong, Lee Stringer, and Kurt Vonnegut, to name a few, together with political titles by voices of conscience, including Subhankar Banerjee, the Boston Women's Health Collective, Noam Chomsky, Angela Y. Davis, Human Rights Watch, Derrick Jensen, Ralph Nader, Loretta Napoleoni, Gary Null, Greg Palast, Project Censored, Barbara Seaman, Alice Walker, Gary Webb, and Howard Zinn, among many others. Seven Stories Press believes publishers have a special responsibility to defend free speech and human rights, and to celebrate the gifts of the human imagination, wherever we can. In 2012 we launched Triangle Square books for young readers with strong social justice and narrative components, telling personal stories of courage and commitment. For additional information, visit www.sevenstories.com.